GIRL THREE:

TRAPPED

(A Maya Gray FBI Suspense Thriller—Book 3)

Molly Black

Molly Black

Debut author Molly Black is author of the MAYA GRAY FBI suspense thriller series, comprising six books (and counting); and the RYLIE WOLF FBI suspense thriller series, comprising three books (and counting).

An avid reader and lifelong fan of the mystery and thriller genres, Molly loves to hear from you, so please feel free to visit www.mollyblackauthor.com to learn more and stay in touch.

BOOKS BY MOLLY BLACK

MAYA GRAY MYSTERY SERIES
GIRL ONE: MURDER (Book #1)
GIRL TWO: TAKEN (Book #2)
GIRL THREE: TRAPPED (Book #3)
GIRL FOUR: LURED (Book #4)
GIRL FIVE: BOUND (Book #5)
GIRL SIX: FORSAKEN (Book #6)

RYLIE WOLF FBI SUSPENSE THRILLER
FOUND YOU (Book #1)
CAUGHT YOU (Book #2)
SEE YOU (Book #3)

CHAPTER ONE

Watching his victims was the most important part of all. He wanted to understand them before he struck, wanted to know every facet of their lives.

Currently, he was watching from inside the van he'd outfitted for exactly that purpose, with a wealth of audio and visual devices feeding information back to him about the outside world.

"...telling you, Marcy, everything's going to be fine. So, do you want to go out Friday night?"

There was a breathy note to Cindy's voice that he'd always disliked, even from the start.

"I can't. I'd have to get a new sitter. Kelly's gone off to college, now."

Of course, he could hear the hesitation in that, the small lie to spare feelings. It was amazing what you could hear, when you only listened hard enough.

"It isn't hard to get a sitter, girl!"

He'd bugged his target's phone, of course. That was simply standard, even if it meant having to put up with banal conversations about whether her friend could get childcare.

He had more bugs in Cindy's handbag, around her house, even placed carefully in one of her shoes, so that wherever she went, he would be able to hear her. Her whole life filtered in through his headphones, focused and amplified until he could pick apart every nuance. The crunch as Cindy ate her morning cereal, the small sound of annoyance as she hung up, telling him exactly what she thought about her friend bailing on her. Since he'd begun his surveillance, he'd heard every tiny sound in her life, come to know her as intimately as a lover.

He could see her too, of course. He'd managed to get a pinhole camera into each of the rooms of her house, letting him watch her movements as well as listen in. Currently, Cindy was sitting in her pajamas, eating cereal and flicking through a well-worn textbook. The rustle of the pages came to him each time she turned them.

She was pretty, he supposed, in that way that youth could so easily be mistaken for prettiness. Cindy had delicate features, a slender frame

1

bordering on the fragile, hair that was getting out of hand already in spite of her having it cut a few days before. He could remember the delicate *snick* of the scissors then, the harsher sound of the hairdryer, and the music in the background.

She went to get dressed, and he looked away from the screen for that part, relying only on his ears. He wasn't a voyeur.

Now she was on the move, and he switched to the driver's seat of the van, keeping his headphones in place. Of course, he had the means to track her by GPS, but sometimes it was better to do things the old-fashioned way.

There was an art to following someone in a van, when they were on foot. Crawling along behind Cindy wouldn't have worked. She would have noticed, would have wondered why there was a creepy van following her so closely. Probably, she would have gotten the license plate, or even made out his face, in spite of the tinted windows.

If she did that, he would have to kill her there on the street, and he didn't want to do that. That wasn't the plan, at all.

The plan was important. The plan was what had kept him safe, doing this.

Instead of creeping along, he skipped ahead of Cindy, starting and stopping, pulling in like he was making deliveries. He actually had a fake ID from a fake delivery company, just in case anyone asked. Not that anyone had. This wasn't a world where people actually *asked,* rather than assuming that it was none of their business. He made a game of it, driving ahead, stopping, listening for Cindy's footsteps as she got closer.

He watched her walk past, letting her go on like an angler playing out the line, then leapfrogged her again in the van to watch and listen once more.

It was hard to stick to the plan on a day like today, when there were so many obvious ways that he could take her. She was barely paying attention to the world around her, certainly didn't notice him or the van in which he sat, except as part of the normal scenery of the city. There were a dozen spots on this route where he could wait for Cindy if he got ahead of her, and where it would be easy to-

No, he had to control himself. It was bad enough that that the chances of discovery were too great here, in daylight. Anyone might walk up. Anyone might catch him in the act, ruining all the secrecy that he'd put so much time and effort into. If they did that, what was he going to do? Kill them too?

Well, yes, obviously. But that depended on them being someone he could overpower; and even if he did so, the commotion might attract still more people to watch. Soon, there would be no chance of containing things, and he would be unveiled, when he'd managed to remain invisible for all this time.

That wasn't all of it, though. There was another layer that mattered almost as much as the simple risk of discovery, perhaps even more. There was a ritual to it by this point, a way of doing things that had worked out perfectly in the past, one that had felt right, and that made sure that no one would ever come close to catching him. It wasn't just sensible to stick to that by this point: it was necessary in a way that even he couldn't fully articulate.

So he let Cindy walk past on her way to work, safe for now, possibly safer than she had ever been in her life. He wasn't going to let anything happen to her now, not before it was *his* chance to act. He would wait, and watch, and listen. He would learn everything there was to learn about her.

It would be the full moon soon enough.

CHAPTER TWO

Maya never thought that she would go back to Pollock, Louisiana; yet here she was, standing outside its prison, just a few days after the last time she'd been there.

She checked her dark suit before she went in and tied back her equally dark hair. She wanted to make sure that she looked presentable, businesslike, for this. Sometimes people looked at her and they saw nothing but a good looking thirty-year-old, maybe a little taller than a lot of women, but with delicate features and a heart shaped face that sometimes made them treat her as if she were younger. Today, she wanted people to see nothing but the agent she was. It helped to distract from the roil of emotions bubbling beneath the surface.

She'd thought that nothing would get her to return, but it turned out that there was one thing: the death of Ade Matheson, the killer she'd found that had also killed prison guard Samantha Neele. The moment she'd heard about his death, Maya had been suspicious. Now it was time to find out if those suspicions were justified.

Maya walked into the reception area, which seemed to be deliberately featureless aside from a large federal corrections logo and a few rows of plastic seating. There was a reception booth behind toughened glass there, with a younger guard in it that Maya recognized as one of those she'd spoken to the last time she was here.

The guard looking after the reception area smiled as Maya came in. It was a big difference from the last time she'd been in Pollock, when it seemed that no one had wanted her.

"Agent Gray," the guard said. "We heard you were coming down, although I'm not sure why."

"I just want to go over the circumstances of Matheson's death for myself," Maya said. "Sorry, I don't think I got your name last time."

"Archer, ma'am."

"I won't take up too much time here, Archer. I just need to take a look at Matheson's cell and talk to anyone he might have interacted with in the time between my leaving and his death."

4

She saw the guard nod. "Yes, of course. The governor said to give you whatever you need. I also just wanted to say thank you."

"You wanted to thank me?" Maya said, not quite understanding.

"For getting rid of Jeremiah. No one wanted him as head guard, but we couldn't do anything about him."

Jeremiah Wood had been the head guard at the prison until Maya's visit. Briefly, she'd even thought that he might be the killer. He hadn't been, but the investigation had turned up enough unpleasantness around him that he'd quickly lost his job and might even be facing charges.

"I'm glad I could help," Maya said, even though, in truth, she hadn't been thinking about the effects on the prison when she'd accused Jeremiah. She'd only been trying to find Samantha Neele's killer in time to appease the man who held her sister and ten other women as hostages.

The Moonlight Killer.

Even now, Maya shuddered at the thought of Megan in the hands of a serial killer. It was a thought that made her want to run screaming to find her, but that wasn't an option, not without information.

That was why she was here. Maya was convinced that the Moonlight Killer had gotten to Ade Matheson somehow.

"I'll take you to see his cell," Archer said.

He led the way through the prison, along gray walled corridors, into wings that smelled stale with the sweat of too many men crammed together for too long. Maya and Archer walked past rows of cells holding inmates in orange jumpsuits. Maya could feel the eyes on her as she passed.

"What you doing here, bitch?"

"Here to be fresh meat for all of us?"

Maya ignored the attempts to intimidate her. She knew that any reaction, from a flinch all the way up to reaching for her gun, would count as a kind of victory to these prisoners.

She made her way along without looking at them, instead taking in the security of the prison. She spotted camera domes at regular intervals, saw the pacing guards on routine patrols that would make sure that they spotted any trouble.

"Do the guards patrol on a fixed pattern?" Maya asked.

Again, Archer nodded. "Yes ma'am, although there are two or three patterns, and we vary them each day, so the prisoners can't get used to when we're coming around."

Maya guessed that would make it harder for them, but not impossible. All it took to work out a pattern like that was time, and prisoners had nothing *but* that.

"Matheson was in the maximum-security wing," the guard said, taking a turning and stopping at a security door with guards standing on either side. "We'll put the whole place on lockdown while you take a look. It wouldn't be safe otherwise."

Maya could hear the note of fear there. She wondered just how bad some of the prisoners had to be to make the guards afraid of them. But then, she didn't *have* to wonder. Ade Matheson had almost killed her when she'd given him only the briefest of chances.

Right then, Maya didn't care about the danger. She almost welcomed it. She'd been feeling on edge ever since the forensics came back on a lock of hair the Moonlight Killer had sent, along with detailed pictures of all the ways he'd hurt one of his bunnies. That hair had belonged to her sister. The thought that he might have done *that* to Megan was too much.

"I still don't get what you're expecting to find," Archer said. "I mean… Matheson hanged himself."

"No," Maya said. "He didn't."

It didn't make any sense for him to have done so. He'd been *sneering* at her about getting caught, telling Maya it would make things better for him in there, not worse. This was a man who was already going to spend the rest of his life in this prison, and yet he'd somehow been found dead in his cell?

The Moonlight Killer had found a way to get to him. It was just a question of proving it.

They moved through into the maximum-security wing, with rows of barred cells that could let guards look inside at any hour of the day or night. Maya saw another camera at the end of the hall, looking out over everything.

"Did the camera catch the moment when he killed himself?" Maya asked. That wasn't really what she was asking. What she was hoping was that there might be footage that no one had looked at, footage that would show the Moonlight Killer slipping in like a ghost. She wanted to see his *face*.

Archer shook his head, though, with an apologetic expression.

"No, ma'am. The camera's down at the moment. Some kind of fault."

"Or it was tampered with," Maya said, but she could see the disbelief on Archer's face.

"Things go wrong, sometimes."

And it was a lot easier to believe that than to think that someone might have taken out the camera prior to moving in to finish off Matheson. Another thought came to Maya: would it be *possible* to tamper with the cameras in here without help? Would it be possible to get into this wing at all? She'd seen the security doors and the guards. Did she really think that someone could just wander in without assistance?

Which meant that the only way it would have been possible for the Moonlight Killer to murder Ade Matheson is if it were an inside job. At least one of the guards had to be in on it for it to work.

Maya found herself glancing across to Archer. She didn't think it was him. Of all the guards there, he was among the friendliest, and it was obvious that he didn't have any time for the things his former colleague Jeremiah had been doing; but she still needed to be careful not to say too much in front of him, just in case.

"This was his cell," Archer said, gesturing to a now empty eight-by-twelve-foot cell, with a bed fixed to the wall and a toilet in the corner. "We found him hanging from the bars. A low-level hanging, using his bed covers."

"And is that how people kill themselves in prison?" Maya asked.

She saw Archer nod. "It's… we try to stop it happening. If they're on suicide watch, we take away anything they might use for it. But… yeah, I've seen it happen before."

It was a reminder of just what a tough job the prison guards could have, but it didn't help Maya to work out exactly what had happened.

"I don't know what you're looking for, really," Archer said. "The guy was facing charges as a serial killer. He was going to spend the rest of his life in prison, so he hanged himself in his cell. It seems simple enough."

Except for the part where Maya didn't believe that Ade Matheson had been in a state of mind where hanging himself had even been a possibility. Matheson was all kinds of things: arrogant, dangerous, convinced of his own superiority, but he wasn't suicidal. Maya would bet anything on that.

Just by coming here, she was betting plenty. The Moonlight Killer had been clear that they shouldn't try to find him.

7

Maya looked around at the cell block. Most of the inmates were locked in their cells, with a few away on work duty or exercising. The eyes of every one of them were fixed on her, and Maya didn't think it was because she was the only woman they'd seen in the flesh in a while. She was sure that they watched *everyone* who came in.

She picked the cell opposite Matheson's, on the basis that the inmate there would have had the best view. He was a weaselly looking Latino man, slender and maybe her age, with tattoos on his neck and face proclaiming his association with some gang or other.

"What do you want?" he snapped at her as Maya came closer.

"What did you see when Ade Matheson died?" Maya asked.

"Just his old white ass, hanging from the door." The prisoner seemed quite pleased with himself for that comment. He pushed up close against the bars. "How about you let me out of here, and I'll show you a good time?"

"How about you tell me who came to his cell?" Maya said. "You saw someone, right?"

"Maybe I did, maybe I didn't. You think I'm talking to some Fed in front of everyone here? Snitches get stitches, lady."

He smirked as he said it. He was enjoying this far too much.

Maya wasn't enjoying it at all. She could feel her frustration building. Her sister was in danger, and this might be the one chance she had to find real information leading to the man who held her. Yet here was this prisoner, acting like it was all a joke. Maya felt something inside her on the verge of snapping. She'd been under too much pressure for too many days now, barely able to sleep knowing that Megan was in the hands of some madman. To know that it was a serial killer only made it worse. As for the photos he'd sent…

Maya knew she should step back, take a breath, slow down, but she couldn't, not now.

"Who did you see?" Maya repeated, stepping almost as close to the bars as the prisoner was.

"You know what you can do, lady? You can die, bitch!"

Maya saw movement from his hand, saw the shiv there in it as it blurred forward. Of course in a place like this, the prisoners would have no problem with trying to kill a stranger.

Maya reacted on instinct, both hands going down to the attacking arm. Maya managed to grab the arm that held the shiv just in time, stopping it before the weapon could punch into her.

8

She slammed it against the cell door, once, then again, jamming it against the bars for leverage. She heard bone snap. The prisoner screamed, letting go of his weapon.

Maya should have stopped there, but the problem with stepping so close to the edge was that it was so easy to slip over it.

Maya grabbed for the prisoner, jerking him face first against the bars as if she might pull him through them. She used one arm to wrap around the back of his neck, pulling him tight, then drove the other arm into his throat from the front. It was a crude choke, but an effective one.

"You think I have time for games?" Maya demanded. "You think I'm going to stop? I've had enough of this. Tell me what you know. Tell me what you saw!"

She could feel Archer trying to pull her off the prisoner, but Maya kept her grip. She loosened it only a fraction, letting him speak.

"Tell me!" she snarled at him. She was going too far, but right then, she didn't care. Megan was in danger, and she was done playing nice.

"Eddie!" the prisoner gasped out. "Eddie Chavez. Used to be locked up here. Gun running or something. He came in, and he was wearing a guard's uniform. He did it, I swear… oh God, my arm!"

Maya let go of him, let Archer pull her off the prisoner. She could see him looking at her like he was almost as afraid of her as of the prisoners, then.

Maya didn't care. She had a name. She had a place to start looking for the Moonlight Killer, and for her sister.

CHAPTER THREE

Maya knew there wasn't any time to waste in tracking down Eddie Chavez. She didn't even call the lead through to Harris, her boss at the FBI.

Part of that was because she wanted to make sure that the kidnapper didn't hear about it. So far, the kidnapper had been one step ahead of her with every move she made. He was *definitely* monitoring police scanners, so why not her communications with her bosses?

A bigger part was that she didn't want to answer any questions about exactly how she'd gotten the information. Maya had gone too far back in the prison, and she knew it. Ok, so the inmate had tried to stab her, but once the shiv had been on the ground, she should have shoved him back. She certainly shouldn't have dragged him into a chokehold to get information out of him.

The need to protect her sister was pushing her to do things she would never normally consider. The worst part about it? Maya would do it all over again if it meant that she got the same information. If it meant getting Megan back safely, she would do *far* more.

Maya went to her car and checked her laptop. She still had the parole files for the prison from her last case, which meant that there was no need to call this in, or to risk an open search on the FBI's system. Once, Harris might have let her go off on her own way, but Maya suspected that now he would want to know every detail of this. He would probably organize another raid, even though the kidnapper had easily managed to avoid those so far.

Thankfully, the parole files gave Maya an address for Eddie Chavez. It was down in Alexandria, just half an hour from the prison. Maya set off, not willing to waste another moment when she could have the Moonlight Killer in her hands.

Was this man the Moonlight Killer? He'd come into the prison and killed Matheson, which only the Moonlight Killer had a reason to do. Yet he'd also been in prison for several years, and that presented an obvious problem. The Moonlight Killer had still been active during that time.

So *not* the Moonlight Killer. The disappointment of that thought was quickly replaced by curiosity. What was Eddie then? The hired help? An accomplice? Someone who might be able to lead Maya to him? It seemed obvious by now that the Moonlight Killer had to have *some* help, or he wouldn't be able to deliver the postcards so quickly, yet this went far beyond a simple delivery.

As Maya drove into Alexandria, she considered what she was about to do. The man she was going to take down had already proven that he was a killer, and if he'd gone to prison on gunrunning charges, there was every chance that he would be armed. Even so, Maya didn't call for backup. She needed to be the one who did this.

She arrived at Eddie's address, which turned out to be a run-down workshop for motorcycles with far too much junk abandoned out front. Maya parked in front of the place, looking it over. There were a lot of potential escape routes here. There was also the possibility that there might be far more people than just Eddie at home. Maya needed to get her hands on Eddie before he knew what was happening.

Making a decision, she walked straight in, doing her best not to look threatening. The workshop had a couple of hydraulic lifts, a few stands for bikes, and a lot of tools lying around. One man was working at the heart of it: a thickset Latino man of about forty, with slicked back hair and hands covered in grease. He was wearing gray overalls with "Eddie's Custom Bikes" printed on the back.

"Excuse me," Maya said.

The man looked around at her. "Can I help you, lady?"

"I hope so," Maya said. "My boyfriend... it's his birthday soon, and he really, really loves custom motorbikes. I was thinking about getting him one, and when I asked around, people kept saying that Eddie did the best ones in Alexandria."

"Not just Alexandria," the man said, the pride obvious on his face. "I do the best bikes in all Louisiana."

"So *you're* Eddie?" Maya said.

"That's me. And you are?"

Maya got out her badge and her gun in one movement. "Agent Gray, FBI. Don't move."

He ignored her, diving for the bench of tools. Too late, Maya saw a handgun there among the rest of it, kept just out of sight behind a toolbox.

Her training said in that moment that she should shoot. Maya overrode the instinct, because if she killed Eddie like this, there would be no one left to give her answers. Instead, she took a charging step forward and stomp kicked him, full force, in the gut.

He was off balance enough that the kick managed to knock him down, and in an instant, Maya was after him.

Eddie was up, though, running through his workshop. This time, he didn't seem to be trying to get to his gun so much as simply get away.

Maya set off in pursuit, hurdling over a partially completed street bike and accelerating. Eddie ducked through a door at the back, and Maya followed.

She saw a flash of something coming the other way and she ducked just in time as a baseball bat passed over her head. Eddie swung it once again, and Maya stepped inside the swing this time, deliberately moving in the opposite direction to the one he would expect. She hit him with an elbow shot, then with the butt of her gun, feeling the hard connection on bone each time.

Still, Eddie was fighting back. He bulldozed into her, grabbing for her gun arm. Maya hit him again to break the grip and saw her chance. Hooking a leg around his, she tripped him, sending him crashing to the floor. She landed on top of him, one knee in his sternum, with the gun pressed into his temple.

"I said, don't move."

This time, he went still.

"What's this even about?" Eddie demanded.

"You know what. Ade Matheson."

Maya saw the reaction, the sudden fear there. She actually thought that Eddie might try to bolt again. That was good, because it meant confirmation that she'd gotten the right man and hadn't been sent on some wild goose chase.

"Who sent you to kill him?" Maya demanded.

"He said… he said there was no way I'd be caught," Eddie said. "He said that he'd arranged it all."

"*Who?*" Maya demanded, grinding the muzzle of the gun into Eddie's skull. "Give me a name!"

Eddie looked panicked then. He'd obviously seen the desperation on Maya's face. There wasn't a trace of doubt there that she would pull the trigger. Good.

"I don't *have* a name! He just sent me this… this *postcard*."

12

Maya stopped. It sounded far too familiar to be a lie.

"What postcard?"

"It... It had my mom's address on it. It told me what to do, and when. It said if I did it, I'd have enough money to get things back together with the shop; and if I didn't, my mom... he threatened to kill my mom."

In that moment, he didn't seem like a tough bad guy anymore, just like someone scared.

"Show me," Maya said.

"What?"

"Show me the postcard!"

"Ok, ok!"

Maya let him up, keeping the gun on him while he fetched it from where it sat, in the middle of a desk, like an accusation. Maya took it carefully. She had evidence bags in her pocket, so she slid it into one carefully, hoping against hope that the Moonlight Killer might not have been as careful with forensics when he was sending a postcard to someone who *wasn't* in the FBI.

The contents were in Spanish, but Maya saw the familiar bunny motif on the front. It wasn't just for her, apparently. She had something now, at least.

"Eddie Chavez, you're under arrest for the murder of Ade Matheson."

*

Maya walked into the FBI HQ with Eddie walking in front of her. She could have left him in Alexandria at their local precinct, but she hadn't wanted to give away the only connection they had to the Moonlight Killer so quickly. It was better to drag him all the way back to D.C. than risk him getting lost in the system somewhere else, especially when Maya was now convinced that the Moonlight Killer had connections on the inside in Pollock.

Maya took him up to the fourth floor, then pushed him out into the bullpen in front of her. Around her, agents were working on a slew of different cases, but the evidence board for *this* case was front and center now, the two cases so far pinned on it in full view in the hope that someone would be able to make a connection.

Deputy Director Harris came out from his office as Maya came in with Eddie. He was well dressed and avuncular, balding, with features that looked down home and forgiving right up to the point where someone got on his bad side. He was wearing a sports jacket over his shirt today rather than a full suit.

"Gray! Who is that? What have you been doing?"

Maya brought Eddie over to her boss. "This is Eddie Chavez, the man who killed Ade Matheson."

"The man who…," Maya could see Harris trying to catch up. It didn't take him long. Staying on top of things was a big part of why he was the boss. "I thought Matheson was supposed to have killed himself."

"He didn't," Maya said, wanting to make that part of it clear from the outset. "Eddie here crept into the prison wearing a guard's uniform, the cameras were all turned off for him, and he strangled Matheson in his cell."

Again, Maya had the feeling of Harris fitting pieces together, seeing the implications of everything that Maya had just said.

"And he did this because…"

"Because someone sent him a postcard."

"Damn it."

Maya could see the frustration on her boss's face.

"Reyes!" he called out. "Take this bastard down to holding. I want to question him. Gray, my office, now!"

Maya followed Harris through to his office, where his tactical vest and FBI jacket hung from an old-fashioned hat stand, and his desk had a green leather top that put Maya in mind of a banker's desk. Harris sat down behind that desk, and Maya shut the door behind her.

It was a while before Harris said anything.

"Why is this the first I'm hearing of all of this, Gray?" Harris demanded.

Maya tried to keep her face neutral. "Sir?"

"Do you think I'm stupid?"

"No, sir," Maya said. That was the last thing Maya thought about her boss.

"So don't play dumb. It took you time to work out that Ade Matheson didn't kill himself. More time to go back to… where was it? Louisiana? There, you found out that this guy was involved in

Matheson's murder? And at *no* point in all of this did you think to call in what you'd found? You didn't call for backup?"

"There was no time," Maya said.

Harris gave her a baleful look. "There was *plenty* of time, but you chose not to fill us in. You chose not to contact us."

Maya couldn't tell her boss the truth then: that she'd thought Harris and the others would hold her back, so she'd left them out of it, before they got her sister killed.

"I work better alone, Sir."

"No, you don't." Harris said. "The FBI isn't a one-woman operation, Gray, and if you do something like that again, you'll find yourself suspended, while the rest of us cover this case."

"But you can't do that!" Maya exclaimed.

"Can't? Last I heard, I was a deputy director," Harris said. "We're a team, Gray, and you need to start being a team player."

Maya knew she should feel chastened by that, but still, she couldn't feel anything but happy that she'd brought Chavez in. She had a starting point from which to look for the Moonlight Killer.

Now, she just needed to get to him, before his sick games killed her sister.

CHAPTER FOUR

Maya sat at her desk, trying and failing to make sense of the Moonlight Killer's cases. She had the files stacked up beside her, and the stack of cases that potentially had some connection to him was as high as her head.

It made for frustratingly slow going. Maya opened a file and scanned through it. This one had a victim who had been shot twice in the head, in what seemed to Maya to be an obvious gangland execution, yet because it had occurred on the night of the full moon, and because it was unsolved, someone somewhere had added a note about a possible connection to the Moonlight Killer.

The next was a young woman who had been strangled on the full moon up in Northampton, Massachusetts, which seemed much more plausible. So did one who had been strangled in the woods of West Virginia.

The trouble was that there were far too *many* that seemed plausible. Ok, so there were some cases, like the older man who had been repeatedly stabbed over in Rhode Island, that were clearly there just because the murder had happened on the night of the full moon, but there were far too many more that might have been the Moonlight Killer or might not have been.

Reyes came over. He was an eager young Latino man, always dressed perfectly, with the hungry eyes of someone determined to go far in the FBI. Maya couldn't deny that he was a good, effective agent, but recently, he'd been poking his nose into this case far too much. Reyes had been the one to suggest focusing on catching the kidnapper rather than solving the first case he'd sent. Reyes had been the one behind the abortive raid on a perfume factory. Now, Maya could see that same eagerness to do the case his way in his eyes.

"Why do you have all the files out on the Moonlight Killer?" Reyes asked.

"How do you know they're the Moonlight Killer files?" Maya countered.

"Because I went down to records and asked for a couple. I wanted to see where the Moonlight Killer fits into all of this."

"Well, what do you think *I'm* doing?" Maya asked him, because it was a lot simpler to say that than to come out with the full truth of why she was doing this. So far, she'd managed to keep her suspicion, her near certainty, that the Moonlight Killer was the kidnapper from Harris and the others. Letting Reyes know would blow that in an instant.

"You need a hand?" Reyes asked.

"Sure," Maya said, because being defensive would only make him suspicious. "I thought I'd start by trying to sort the wheat from the chaff with these, work out which ones are actually likely to have been Moonlight Killer cases."

"Because the two you were sent to investigate so far have been ones that didn't turn out to be him?"

That was the thing with Reyes, with anyone here: it was important not to underestimate how sharp they were. They didn't get to be FBI agents by being stupid.

"You reckon this kidnapper is hunting the Moonlight Killer?" Reyes said. "He's going to keep throwing you at cases until you find him?"

"Maybe." Actually, Maya didn't think that at all. She thought that the Moonlight Killer was trying to weed out the crimes that weren't his, trying to claim a kind of credit by process of elimination.

"So, what are you looking for? The ones that are most likely to be him?"

Maya shook her head. "I figure if we try to eliminate the least likely, that's all we can do. We don't know enough about the Moonlight Killer to say for certain that one crime or another is his."

That was the biggest problem with this most elusive of serial killers: there was no knowing what was true and what wasn't. Maya *thought* that cases without strangulation probably weren't his. She thought that he preferred a ligature to manual strangulation. Yet it was all supposition. For all Maya knew, all the cases that she had down as not belonging to the Moonlight Killer because they were shootings or stabbings were his, and half the strangulations weren't.

It was hard, too, doing the work that she needed to do with Reyes looking over her shoulder. From the way he'd behaved with the raid, it was obvious that Reyes was looking to swoop in on any success Maya had, jumping ahead to his own conclusions in the hope of being the one to close this case. Unlike Maya, it was pretty obvious that Reyes had promotion ambitions.

All of it meant that simply going through the files at her desk wasn't going to do a lot of good. Maya worked better alone.

More than that, she was starting to think that she was looking at this the wrong way. There was no way of knowing which murders were down to the Moonlight Killer, but Maya knew a series of crimes for sure that he *had* been involved in.

Making a decision, Maya grabbed the three or four files that might actually help her with this and headed for the door.

"If Harris wants me, I'll be at home."

*

Home had never been very homey. Maya's apartment had always been more of a base from which to head out in different directions than the place she wanted to spend all of her time. Now, it was made even less cozy by the evidence boards Maya was starting around the walls.

Pictures of dead women stared back at Maya, with Anne Postmartin and Samantha Neele's eyes on her as she worked. Maya had set up newspaper clippings around them, and fragments of casefiles, along with her own sticky notes, trying to see something there.

Maya had put them on a separate wall from the others, because the Moonlight Killer hadn't murdered either one of them. Yet he'd picked those two cases out of all the potential false positives out in the world, all the cases where people *thought* it had been him at their heart. Maybe working out why would help with that.

Maya pinched the bridge of her nose. What did Samantha Neele and Anne Postmartin have in common, other than the fact that people had thought they were killed by the Moonlight Killer? Was there anything else about them?

If there was an extra connection there, Maya couldn't see it yet.

She went down to her mailbox, partly to give herself some time to think, partly because it had become a habit by now. She checked the mail reflexively, not wanting to miss the possibility that a postcard might have been delivered with another case for her to solve. If a case did arrive, it would come with a deadline, and Maya didn't want to waste a single minute of that time.

18

There was nothing this time, so she headed back up, taking the stairs two at a time. Maya didn't know what her neighbors thought of her doing this. She barely spoke to them. She preferred things that way.

Back in her apartment, Maya turned to the other wall. This one had details of the women Maya knew the Moonlight Killer had taken: Liza Carty, Gabi Dubov, Megan Gray. Her sister's face sat there between the other two, and Maya tried to look for any similarities that might give her a way into the Moonlight Killer's mind.

She needed to profile him, but there was little enough to go on. It was obvious from the kidnappings that he preferred to target women. Even Eddie Chavez had found his mother threatened rather than a brother or his father. Was that just because he thought the women in question were the most effective leverage against people, or was it because he had a preferred victim type, and he'd grabbed for them automatically when he'd been collecting his "bunnies?"

Why did he call them bunnies? Was that just a reference to them being kept underground somewhere, or did it point to some deeper pathology?

Looking at the three on the wall, it was obvious that they had certain facial similarities. They were all young, all pretty, and crucially, all pretty in the same fine boned kind of way. Maybe the Moonlight Killer really *did* have a type.

What else could Maya tell about him based on what she'd learned from the activities of the kidnapper? Did she learn anything else when she fed in the realization that the kidnapper was the Moonlight Killer?

Maya looked around the room, and she knew how all of this would look to any of her colleagues who saw it. They would think that she was getting obsessed, that she was getting too caught up in all of this because of her sister. What else was she supposed to do, though? Was Maya meant to just sit back and wait for someone like Reyes to bring Megan back to her? No, *she* had to be the one to solve all of this.

Even the Moonlight Killer thought so, or why else would he send her the postcards?

Now that Maya had thought about them, she had to go downstairs to check again. Still, there was nothing but the usual detritus of bills and fast-food menus. Grabbing one at random, she headed upstairs and ordered takeout. Maya didn't even really care what it was. Nothing else mattered except the case.

What did she know?

She knew that the Moonlight Killer had targeted young women as his "bunnies." Maya had thought that there might be a performance connection, but Gabi Dubov disproved that. It had to be something else.

She knew that the Moonlight Killer was clever, obviously high functioning, simply to avoid being caught for so long. She knew now that he liked games. His focus on rules to be followed told her that he was an orderly, not disorderly, serial killer, which might help to rule out some of the other crimes attributed to him.

What else?

The fact that he'd used claymore mines as traps might point to some kind of military training, which might also be backed up by the way he was able to strike without being seen. Given the way he seemed to know everything about Maya's life, maybe some kind of background in intelligence work was a possibility. Of course, it could just be someone who'd always *wanted* to do that kind of work, too, but there was something about the precision with which all of this had been executed that made Maya think of military intelligence.

Was that why he'd picked her? Did he think they were similar?

What else?

Maya went down to check for postcards again as she asked herself that question, the way she checked far too often *every* day.

The most obvious point now was the realization that the Moonlight Killer didn't work alone. That was a big shift in understanding him. Every investigation before had assumed that he was a solitary killer, and maybe he still was for that part of things, but it was also clear that he was more than capable of using other people. He had someone, maybe more than one someone, deliver the postcards. He'd found ways to get Eddie Chavez into the prison. He'd been able to blackmail Eddie into murdering for him.

What else?

That was the problem, though: sooner or later, Maya ran up against the limits of supposition. She'd guessed more about the Moonlight Killer today than most people had in years, but finding proof for it, or using any of it to narrow things down to a single name? That was still a long way off.

Maya seethed in frustration at her inability to do anything with what she'd found. She was still seething when her phone went off, announcing a text that turned out to be from Marco Spinelli, the Cleveland detective who'd worked with her on her last two cases.

You said you wanted to get dinner the next time we were in the same town. Well, I'm in D.C. Dinner in an hour?

That caught Maya completely off guard. Despite how hot things had blown between them when they'd worked together, she'd hardly heard anything from him since. Not that she'd been the one reaching out to make contact either. She'd been too busy.

Maya almost texted back to say that she was too busy for this, too, yet something stopped her. Part of it was the fact that she did want to see Marco again. Part of it was the knowledge that if she didn't get out of her apartment soon, she would probably sit there forever, obsessing.

Part of it was the thought that if anyone would understand what was going on right then, it was Marco. Maybe *he* would be able to work all of this out.

I'll be there, Maya texted back.

CHAPTER FIVE

From the moment Maya walked into the restaurant, Marco knew that the trouble he'd gone to over tonight was worth it.

There had been quite a bit of trouble. First, there was the fact that he'd had to come up to Washington from Cleveland. He'd swung it with his bosses by finding a training course here on case management protocols, but still had to drive up in Betsy, his beaten-up old Explorer. He'd had to get a hotel room. He'd researched D.C. restaurants to find one that was nice, but not so fancy that it would make him and Maya uncomfortable to be there. He'd settled on a pleasant little Italian restaurant, with booths set around the walls, gentle lighting, and what looked like good reviews. Then he'd had to actually get a reservation, in a city where it seemed that people spent almost as much time fighting over that kind of thing as they did over politics.

Marco had dressed up, but not too much. He was wearing a clean shirt, dark slacks, and one of his better jackets. He suspected that the last thing Maya wanted him to be was some smoothly suited D.C. guy.

Then he saw her and wished that he'd dressed up more. She was wearing a dark dress that hugged her figure, with a black jacket thrown over the top. Her hair was hanging loose for once, flowing around the lines of her face. She looked completely different, but definitely not in a bad way.

"Maya, it's so good to see you," Marco said, moving forward to greet her. He realized about halfway that he wasn't *sure* how to greet her, at least, not here. Did he shake her hand? Hug her?

"You too, Marco," Maya replied. She seemed to be having the same problem with the whole greeting issue that Marco was. They resolved it by taking their seats and ordering.

"Wine?" Marco asked.

"Definitely."

There was something about the way Maya said it that caught Marco's attention.

"Rough day?"

He saw Maya take a long gulp of her wine. "You could say that. I caught Ade Matheson's killer."

That caught Marco completely by surprise. "You did *what*?"

"I took a trip back to the prison, found an inmate who saw who'd killed him, went to Alexandria, caught him, and brought him back," Maya said.

She made it all sound so simple.

"You just went and *did* all that?" Marco said.

"Now you sound like my boss."

"That's the last thing I want to sound like," Marco didn't want to sound like *anything* work related right now. "How did… no. I don't want to just talk about work. I want to hear more about you."

Several seconds of silence followed.

"I'm sorry," Marco said. "That makes this sound like some kind of job interview."

"Don't be sorry. It's just, at the moment, it's pretty much all work." Maya didn't look entirely comfortable. "It's… it's Megan."

"I know," Marco said. He understood what she was going through probably as well as anyone. "I get that you're worried, but maybe, just for one night, you need to unwind."

He saw Maya nod. "I… guess so."

He saw her take another sip of wine, and as their starters arrived, they both dove into them. Well, he did. Maya picked at hers, which seemed strange, because he'd seen her with a good appetite before.

"What was it like for you growing up?" Marco asked her, wanting to talk about something that wasn't either of their jobs.

"It was good," Maya said. "Megan and I would always…"

She tailed off.

"Sorry," Marco said. "I didn't think."

"No," she replied. "*I'm* sorry. It should… it should be easier than this."

It should. Back in Cleveland, everything had been so easy between them. They'd seemed to connect on a level that Marco hadn't expected. Then, in Louisiana, the only thing that had kept more from happening between them was the fact that Marco hadn't wanted to let anything personal happen between them while they were still working together.

Even though they weren't working together now, it seemed that work was still in the way. The whole, dreadful situation that Maya was in sat there like an extra, unwanted guest in the background.

Marco guessed that they could keep trying to push through, trying to ignore it all, but the whole evening would just end up stilted. He'd been hoping for some grand date, a chance to sweep Maya off her feet, but it was already clear that wasn't going to happen.

The only thing he could do now was try to be there for her anyway. Maybe there would be another chance at some point in the future. Marco picked at his main course as it arrived.

"Tell me about it all," he said. "You know I'll help if I can."

"The man who has my sister is the Moonlight Killer."

Those words were the *last* thing Marco had been expecting to hear this evening, but then he hadn't expected the evening to go in this kind of direction at all. He'd known that they would say a couple of brief things about work, but then he'd assumed that they would go on to just talking about one another, getting to know one another, enjoying their date.

It was hard to do any of that after what he'd just heard.

"You're sure?"

"It's the only explanation that makes sense," Maya said. "The kidnapper has me looking to correct the record on which crimes the Moonlight Killer has committed, and which he hasn't. This isn't some other killer trying to find him, or he'd have sent me on cases that were actually his. It's *him*, Marco."

The enormity of that started to hit Marco then, while Maya took another long gulp of her wine.

"You should take it easy on that," Marco said.

Maya shook her head. "That's the last thing I need. I need to block this out, or I'm not going to be able to sleep tonight."

She sounded as if she didn't sleep most nights.

"I'm tired, Marco. So... tired."

Maya actually looked as if she might cry in that moment and, from her, that was almost the most shocking thing of all. Marco had seen how tough she was, and how hard she worked not to show the kind of emotion that someone else might use against her.

The idea that the Moonlight Killer might be the one who had Maya's sister explained a lot of that. It explained why she looked as if she were right on the edge, barely holding it together in spite of how tough she was.

"Do your bosses know all this?" Marco asked.

24

Maya gave him a look of pure disbelief. "Can you *imagine* how they would react if they knew? It would be a circus. You remember what it was like when they thought that he'd killed Anne Postmartin?"

Marco remembered, better than anyone. He'd been the one who had wanted to pursue other angles, while FBI agents and his own department had run this way and that after the Moonlight Killer. A circus was the right term for it.

He could imagine that circus now, and how quickly the women the Moonlight Killer held would be disregarded. He understood why Maya hadn't told them; but even so, it seemed like a lot to hold in.

"You can't keep all of this to yourself, Maya," he said. "Just look at you. It's eating you up. Tonight... I hoped tonight could be something between us."

"I'm sorry," Maya said, and those words hurt Marco as much as the rest of it. He didn't mean to make her feel worse about all this. He hadn't even meant to say what he just did.

He hadn't come to D.C. to hurt her.

"You don't need to be sorry," he said. "But I'm worried about you. You don't have anyone to talk to about all of this."

"I have you," Maya pointed out, and then paused, taking another drink and looking less confident than Marco had seen her. "I *can* talk to you about all this?"

"Yes, of course you can," Marco said, because what else was he going to say? He wasn't going to leave Maya to cope with this alone.

"I've been trying to work on this," Maya said, "building a profile, trying to work out more about him. I was doing it when you texted. It's so... frustrating. There are things I can work out, but they seem too general. Based on the way he works, and the tactics he uses, maybe he's former military intelligence, but I have no way of proving it, and even if he is, that could be one of hundreds, maybe thousands, of people."

Even so, it impressed Marco that Maya had managed to work out that much about a man who was otherwise faceless.

"No one else has gotten even that much," Marco said.

Maya shook her head. "It's a guess, nothing more."

"A better guess than I've heard from most other people," Marco said. "You need to trust yourself on this, Maya, but you also... you need to stop pushing yourself so hard."

"If I don't push, people will die, Marco," Maya said, and Marco could tell from her face that she believed it. If she'd taught him one thing, working together, it was that.

"That's...," Marco wanted to try to find a kind way to say it, something empathetic, but he also knew that Maya was an ex-solider. Maybe she *needed* to hear this the hard way. "That's so *arrogant*, Gray."

"Arrogant?"

"You're not the only person in the world who can save your sister. You're not the only one who can help these women. You're part of a team, and you have people around you who want to help."

"You're right, I should-"

"I'm saying none of this is your fault, Maya," Marco said.

That seemed to take Maya by surprise, as if she'd never even considered it.

"If it weren't for me, then my sister wouldn't be-"

"That was the Moonlight Killer's choice, not yours," Marco said. "You didn't choose any of this, and you've done more than anyone could reasonably expect. You've solved two unsolved murders in less than a couple of weeks. You're doing everything you can. You'll get through this."

"What if I don't?" Maya said.

Marco reached out for her hand. "You will."

Maya smiled wanly. "I'm sorry, you went to all this trouble, and all I've done is talk about my problems. Are you ok with calling it a night? Maybe we can try again another time?"

"Once there aren't kidnappings and murders hanging over us?" Marco said. "Yes."

He would definitely prefer it to a night like this. It had gone anything but the way he'd hoped.

He and Maya signaled for the bill, but it wasn't their waiter who came across. Instead, it was the manager, coming over from the front of house with something in his hand.

"Excuse me, you're Maya Gray, right?"

Marco saw Maya nod cautiously, as if expecting that it might be the prelude to some kind of outburst. Marco's own instincts were firing, telling him that something was very wrong, and not just because of the way the date had gone.

"This is going to sound rather strange, but there was a delivery for you."

"A delivery?" Maya said. Marco could hear the surprise in her voice, but also the sudden eagerness. In that moment, he knew that nothing was going to get her to slow down and look after herself.

"Yes, ma'am. This."

He set a postcard down on the table, the front covered in images of bunnies.

CHAPTER SIX

Maya was up out of her seat as soon as she saw the postcard, running towards the door without even having to think about it. A waiter got in her way, obviously thinking that she was trying to run out on the bill, but Maya sidestepped him.

She almost tripped over the heels she was wearing, kicked them off, and kept running in bare feet. It didn't matter, if only she could catch up to whoever had brought the card, she might have another avenue to get to the Moonlight Killer.

Maybe it was even him. Maybe he was doing *this* part personally. Maya sprinted out into the street, feeling the coldness of the sidewalk under her feet as she looked around in every possible direction to try to spot the person who had delivered the postcard.

There were people out there, of course, out in the evening walking to one of the city's nightspots, or maybe coming home from a busy day at the office. Was it one of them? If so, how was Maya supposed to be able to pick out the Moonlight Killer from among them all? He could be watching now, standing among the crowds of people and laughing at her attempts to seek him out.

Maya looked around for anyone watching, but the problem with that was that now *everyone* was watching. They were looking at the strange woman who had come running out of a restaurant in bare feet, staring around as if trying to spot someone who wanted to kill her.

The frustration of that was enormous, with the knowledge that she could be looking right at the Moonlight Killer and not know it burning inside her. Not that it had to be the Moonlight Killer. It could just be someone he'd forced into acting as a courier for him. Possibly even just a paid courier, since he would have had plenty of time to set it up after Maya and Marco arranged to go to the restaurant.

Maya stood there breathing hard, trying to calm down. She had to turn around and walk back into the restaurant, finding Marco there, arguing with a couple of the waiters and the manager, who weren't letting him pass.

"I'm telling you that I'm a cop and this is an emergency situation!"

"I'm sure, sir, but the bill needs to be settled *first*."

Maya walked over, shaking her head. "It's too late. If he was here at all, he's gone now."

She saw Marco relax a little, backing away towards their seats. Maya picked up her shoes, ignoring the disapproving looks of the wait staff and customers as she put them on again. She went to the table and picked up the postcard by its corners. She didn't have any evidence bags on her tonight, but by this point it was obvious that the Moonlight Killer was careful not to leave any traces on the cards anyway.

"Do you even have your gun on you tonight?" Marco asked.

Maya shook her head absently. She'd come out without it, because this was a date, not work. Not that it had turned out that way. She hadn't been able to stop herself.

"So you ran out there, potentially after a serial killer, without a weapon?"

Maya could hear the worry there in Marco's tone. Maya could understand it. If anyone else had done what she'd done, she would have told them it was completely the wrong thing to do. This *wasn't* someone else, though.

"My sister's in danger," Maya said. "I had to take the risk."

"And will it save her if you get killed?" Marco replied.

Maya knew that he had a point, but even so, she couldn't bring herself to accept it. If the same thing happened again, she would still run outside, looking for who had brought the postcard in the crowd.

It hadn't paid off, but maybe soon it would. For now, there was only the postcard. Maya stared at it. There were only ten bunnies on the front now, lined up in little hutches as if to emphasize their captivity. On the back was the by now familiar handwriting of the Moonlight Killer. Could *that* prove to be useful evidence? Could it be used to link other writing to him?

Maybe, assuming that it was him, and not another of his "bunnies" being forced to write for him the way he'd made her sister write in the past. And assuming that Maya could get other samples somewhere to compare it to.

For now, its contents were the main focus.

Congratulations on your last case, Maya. I have another for you. Jenette Hiatt. You have until the night of the full moon, or not just one woman dies, but two.

The night of the full moon? That was only three days away! It wasn't even close to enough time to do everything that Maya knew would need to be done. It meant that there wasn't an instant to lose.

"I need to go," Maya said. "I have to get to HQ. I have to get started on this right away."

"Now?" Marco said, sounding as though he couldn't quite believe it.

"There's no time for anything else. Come with me?"

Marco was already shaking his head, though. "I can't. I have to be back in Cleveland first thing tomorrow. You're on your own for this one, Maya."

On her own. Well, she'd been on her own plenty of times before. Until Marco had come along, the thought of working with a partner had just seemed ludicrous. She could handle this. She *would* handle this.

"That's ok," Maya said. "Do you think the waiters will stop me if I rush out again?"

"I'll get the bill," Marco said. "Don't worry about it."

Maya could hear the disappointment there in his voice. He'd obviously been hoping for far more from tonight. Honestly, so had she, and it hurt that she'd messed things up by talking about work, and her sister, so much. But right now, that was the most important thing in her life. She had to focus on this.

She had a new case now, and only three days to find an answer.

*

Maya rushed into the FBI office. She'd taken the time to rush home, change, and pack a bag, but now she found herself resenting every second that she had to spend on it. Maya hurried up to the fourth floor, finding most of the lights off in the bullpen, because who stayed this late if they weren't in the middle of working on a case?

"Gray? What are you doing here?"

Trust Harris to be in, whatever the hour. The deputy director seemed to practically live here. Maybe he did, for all she knew.

"There's been a new postcard, sir," Maya said. She went over to her desk and the deputy director followed her. Most of the files she'd brought out were still there. It seemed that Reyes had gotten bored with going through them after a while.

"Show me," Harris instructed.

Maya handed over the postcard while she started hunting through the piles for the file she needed. She saw Jenette Hiatt's name and pulled the file out, only barely keeping the stack above from collapsing.

"This came to your apartment again?" Harris said. "We need to think about getting a team to watch it, see if we can pick up who delivers these things."

"This wasn't my apartment," Maya said. She opened the file, starting to read. "I was out for dinner."

A glance up caught Harris's look of concern.

"That's bad, Gray. It means that this kidnapper is tracking you wherever you go. We already know that he's dangerous."

He didn't know *how* dangerous, because Maya hadn't told him who the postcard sender was yet. Still, he would have seen the reports of the booby traps in the raid locations, would *definitely* have heard about the men who had been caught in them.

"He told us at the start of this that he would be watching," Maya said.

"Hmm... maybe we can work out some kind of counter-surveillance, pick him up while he watches you. At the very least, we can try to stop him from seeing everything you do."

On another day, Maya might have jumped at that chance. She hated the thought that the Moonlight Killer was watching everything she did somehow. Even so, she had to shake her head.

"We've already seen what happens when we go looking for him, sir," Maya said. "People get hurt, and he escalated his 'warnings' about the women last time by hurting one of them."

He'd sent detailed photos of the injuries he'd inflicted, cataloguing every one as if to make it clear that it was their fault. The lock of hair that had come with detailed photos had been her sister's. Just the thought of all those injuries being inflicted on Megan was enough to make Maya feel sick.

"We can't just let him play this his way forever," Harris said.

"For now, we have to," Maya said. "We don't even know if he's listening in to this conversation."

"In the middle of the FBI headquarters, Gray?"

Maya knew how paranoid that had to sound. "For now, I want to focus on the case."

"Tell me the details," Harris said, still staring at the postcard as if it might give him some answers

31

"Jenette Hiatt, 33. Killed a year ago in Corvallis, Oregon, on the night of the full moon. She was strangled and left to be found on one of the fairways of the local golf club. The unit dedicated to the Moonlight Killer looked at the case, and the file is open, but it looks as though it was left through a lack of evidence."

There was a picture of her as she'd been in life. She had angular features accentuated by close cropped dark hair and facial studs. A couple of tattoos worked their way up her arms.

"They knew it was the Moonlight Killer, but there wasn't any evidence to find him," Harris said.

"Assuming it's him. The last two weren't."

"Reyes told me your theory that it might be someone trying to catch him," Harris said. "Maybe we'll get lucky, and this will give us the information we need to bring him in. Maybe if we do that, the kidnapper will release all the women in one go."

Maya couldn't tell him how unlikely that was without explaining to Harris exactly what she'd worked out about the kidnapper. He was already too eager to go hunting for him, without figuring out that it was the Moonlight Killer. No, it was better to keep going as things were, at least for now.

"I'll catch a late flight over to Oregon," Maya said. "It will be too late to do anything by the time I get there, but at least I'll be able to get started first thing in the morning."

"You do that," Harris said. "I'll coordinate with their local police department. Maybe for once we can have the local cops actually *cooperate* with you."

Maya would believe that when she saw it. After her last couple of cases, she'd realized just how little local police departments sometimes liked working with the FBI. Particularly, it seemed, on anything involving the Moonlight Killer. They didn't want the publicity. They certainly didn't want anyone coming in and telling them that their original investigations hadn't been good enough.

"I hope so, sir. I don't have enough time this time to deal with another department that tries to shut me down."

Three days wasn't much, especially if it turned out that she was running into hostility. So far, she'd been lucky, because she'd been able to find breaks in the cases that she'd investigated quickly enough to satisfy the Moonlight Killer. Even so, she'd missed the first deadline he gave her by an hour. He'd already said in one of his postcards that he wasn't planning to be generous about that again.

"What's all this about two women dying?" Harris said.

"I don't know, sir," Maya said. "Maybe he's upping the stakes."

"Or maybe he knows something we don't. Maybe the Moonlight Killer is planning to strike again, and he wants you to stop him."

"I'm not sure about that, sir," Maya said.

The only thing she was sure about was that she had to get to Oregon and find answers. If she didn't, then in three days, women were going to die.

CHAPTER SEVEN

Carmel Johnson had never thought of herself as a timid person before the man in the mask took her. She'd always thought of herself as strong and capable, tough, not willing to take crap from anyone. She'd stood up to fences and gang members, knowing that backing down would just get her seen as weak.

Yet now, down in whatever place this was, she found herself shuddering as he came in, going quiet, backing away.

"It's time for you to be shut in your hutches for the night, bunnies."

It wasn't just that he was a large and intimidating man. It wasn't even the stun gun that he kept by his side to strike back at any hint of resistance from them. It wasn't how quick he was to use violence, or the fact that they had no way of knowing whether the women who had gone had really been set free or had simply been murdered by him.

All of those things were terrifying enough, but his eyes were worse.

Those eyes were turned on her now, because Carmel realized that she'd frozen in place. They should have been just normal blue-gray eyes, shouldn't have told her anything about him at all. Instead, though, there was something so cold about them. Something that said he didn't care whether she lived or died, that in fact, he might *prefer* it if she died.

Those were the eyes of a man who might do anything at all to her and the others.

"To your hutch, little bunny."

Carmel ran to the caged off space that was hers. By day, she and the others got to walk around freely, and at first, she'd thought that was a kindness. Now, though, she thought that maybe it was a kind of cruelty, because it just highlighted to all of them how little chance there was of getting out. The only way was through the big, airlock style door at one end of the bunker, and that was watched by those cameras of his, so that there was no chance of even touching it without him reacting.

It was locked, too, although that wasn't such a problem for Carmel. A locked door had always been a challenge, not an insurmountable obstacle.

The "hutch" was a small space with a pallet for sleeping, a bucket, and nothing else. Its door was a barred gate that had probably originally been intended for a garden somewhere but served perfectly well as a prison door. It was closed off by a solid-looking padlock.

Around Carmel, all the other women there hurried back to their cells. Carmel could see them in their identical gray jumpsuits, giving no indication of who they had been before. Most of them were disheveled by this point, all of them were dirt streaked. How long had they been down there? Being locked in for the night gave some shape to the days here, but Carmel had lost count.

"Now, who to choose? Who to choose?" Their masked captor moved among them slowly, singing to himself in that perfect tenor that seemed almost as terrifying as his eyes. "Dear Maya has started another round of our little game, and soon, one of you bunnies either gets released back into the wild or... well, you know what happens if she fails."

If this woman failed at whatever game he was playing with her, then one of them died. That made the whole thing more terrifying, not even having any control over what happened. Carmel could do everything perfectly here, and she could still find herself dragged out to be murdered in front of the others. It was a thought that made her want to wrench at the bars of her cage.

It wasn't like this woman was perfect, either. Oh, two of them had been released, if she could believe even that much from the masked man; but the first time, he'd made it clear that she was late. The second time, she'd done something that had pissed him off so much that he'd...

Without even wanting to, Carmel found herself looking over to where the one he'd hurt squatted in her cell. She was usually almost silent, barely joining in the whispered conversations that the women there managed among themselves. Carmel could respect that. She didn't say much either. She didn't see the point. Just because she was locked up here with these women, that didn't make them her friends.

Her wounds were bandaged now, but Carmel could still make out plenty of bruises, plenty of burns. Her lip was swollen from being hit. Carmel could still remember her screams as he'd done all of that. Carmel didn't want to end up like her.

She wanted to end up dead even less.

The masked man started to move around the room. He paused in front of the injured one.

"Not you, obviously. You're too valuable for that right now."

He moved to the next, pausing to consider in silence.

"No, someone else, I think. This has to be perfect."

Suddenly, he was standing in front of Carmel's cell, looking at her, assessing her like some piece of meat. Those cold eyes roved over her, and it might almost have been better if there had been any spark of reaction there. Carmel knew she was good looking, had tricked plenty of marks by making them think they had a chance with her. Here, there was only an assessment that she couldn't even begin to guess at.

"No, not you," he said after what felt like an eternity.

He turned away from Carmel, and she saw the moment when something fell from his belt. She saw the multi-tool hit the ground, and against the dirt it was almost silent. Even so, she braced herself for him to spin back towards it and pick it up.

He didn't, though. Instead, he moved to another of the women, his back still to her. Barely daring to do it, Carmel reached out through the bars, her fingers at full stretch as she tried to reach the multi-tool.

If he turned back now, she was dead. Even so, Carmel kept reaching, felt the metal of the multi-tool under her fingers, scrabbled for it. Her hand closed over it, and she snatched it back to herself.

"Yes, you," their captor said, standing in front of a young, blonde-haired woman who was so underfed she looked as though she might fall over at any moment.

Carmel quickly stowed her prize inside her jumpsuit, managing it just before the masked man turned around. For a moment, his eyes fell on her, and Carmel was certain that she had messed this up, that he would see exactly what she'd done and punish her for it.

Then he turned and headed for the door.

Carmel breathed a sigh of relief. She felt the coldness of the multi-tool against her. It wasn't perfect for the kind of work she needed to do, but it was a lot better than nothing. She was pretty sure that she'd find a way to get through the locks with it at least.

She had to, if she was going to escape.

The temptation was to do it now, to start working on the lock to her cage straight away. Carmel knew better than that, though. He would be watching through those cameras of his. She had to wait, leave her attempt until the dead of night.

Once she could be sure he was asleep, *then* she could make her attempt.

CHAPTER EIGHT

It was far too early in the morning as Maya pulled up in her rental car outside the police headquarters in Corvallis. Around her, the city wasn't yet awake, although Maya got the feeling that it would be pretty sleepy compared to D.C. even when it got fully going.

A quick web search on the flight over had told her that it was a city of only a little over fifty thousand people, sitting close to its barely larger neighbor Albany near the west coast. It was the sort of city whose tourist sites boasted about the walking and local crafts to be found in the area rather than the major monuments and huge stars to come out of it. The whole place seemed pretty enough, hugging the Willamette River, but it had a much smaller town feel to it than D.C. or Cleveland.

Maya just hoped that the local cops would be friendlier than in the last small town she'd been in.

She walked up the steps to the local precinct. Maya had checked into her hotel, but hadn't slept yet, because with so little time, she needed to get started on this. The precinct was a square, concrete built structure that looked as if aesthetics had been very much secondary to function, and to getting the whole thing done on a budget. There were a few squad cars parked outside even at this hour of the morning. Even in a small city like this, the precinct never closed.

Maya walked in and found a smiling receptionist behind a glass screen, a middle-aged woman who looked far happier and more awake than Maya did right then.

"What can I do for you, ma'am?"

Maya showed her badge. "I'm Agent Gray, with the FBI cold cases unit. My boss should have called to say that I was coming."

She braced herself for the resistance that might follow. After all, the last couple of precincts she'd been in, the bosses there hadn't been happy to see her at all. Either they thought that she was there to undermine their work, or they thought that she would waste a bunch of their time when there were better things to do than chase after serial killers who couldn't be caught.

As such, Maya was quite surprised when the receptionist's smile only widened.

"I just got a message from upstairs to look out for you an hour ago. They said to send you straight up when you got here. Homicide is on the third floor."

The friendliness of it caught Maya by surprise. "Thanks," she said, stumbling over it slightly. "I'd better get up there."

Even this early in the morning, there were cops bringing people in: a couple of drunks who looked as though they'd been in a fight, a young man in a hoodie who struggled with the cop escorting him. Maya made her way past them all to an elevator, punched the button for the third floor, and waited.

She came out into a long corridor with a row of offices on either side, completely different to the bullpen arrangement Maya was used to. To her surprise, there were three cops waiting for her: one man in his fifties, with light gray hair and a slight paunch, a dark haired woman about Maya's age dressed in slacks with her shirt sleeves rolled up above the elbow like she was getting ready for some kind of physical work, and a man a little younger than them all, tall, with sandy blond hair and youthful features that made him look as if he were there on some kind of day release from high school.

"Agent Gray?" the older man said. "I'm Chief Strauss. These are detectives Bennet and Collingwood. They'll be your liaisons on this case. I just wanted to say how important to all of us it is that we play our part in trying to catch the Moonlight Killer. Anything you need, just ask."

"That's... very kind of you," Maya said. It was also completely unexpected.

"The death of Jenette Hiatt was a huge deal here," Chief Strauss said. "The biggest crime to hit this town in decades. You could say that the search for the Moonlight Killer put us on the map."

"Put you on the map?" Maya said, not quite understanding. To her, the police chief sounded as though he was almost grateful for the fact that someone had been killed by a notorious serial killer in his town.

"Do you know how much attention our police department has gotten thanks to this?" Chief Strauss said. "We've even had extra funding for the search. The Moonlight Killer is big news, and that kind of news can only help a department like ours."

Maya felt a little uncomfortable hearing that. It seemed a little… distasteful, being thankful for the possibility that someone had been killed by a serial killer. She also suspected that Chief Strauss wouldn't be so happy if this turned out not to be the Moonlight Killer. *When,* given that the Moonlight Killer seemed to be using Maya to clear up cases that had nothing to do with him.

"Just tell us what you need, and we'll be happy to help," Detective Bennet said. She looked eager to get started. "The hunt for the Moonlight Killer is our top priority for as long as you're here."

Again, that eagerness seemed like a little too much to Maya. She was grateful for the help, but did she really need people obsessed with the Moonlight Killer following her around on this, even if they were cops?

For now, though, she wasn't sure that there was much of a choice.

"The first thing I want is to see the crime scene," Maya said.

Detective Collingwood raised an eyebrow. "Which one?"

*

Maya stood on the city's golf course, looking out over the river as the early morning light reflected off it in a haze of pink and gold. From here, she could see for a mile in any direction, and she could definitely *be* seen, because even at this hour there were golfers staring at them while they played.

"So this is the spot where the body was found?" Maya said.

Bennet and Collingwood stood to either side of her, looking on as if expecting her to perform some kind of FBI wizardry.

"That's right," Bennet said. "A couple of golfers getting in their early morning round found Jenette Hiatt and called the death in."

"And their statements?" Maya said.

"They didn't say much, didn't see anything," Collingwood said. "We'll give you full access, of course."

Of course, as if that was what every other department did. Maya wasn't used to that level of cooperation without fighting for it. It would have been good, except for the lingering feeling that the cops here enjoyed their city being the center of attention a little too much.

"So this was the site where the killer chose to display Jenette," Maya said. "How *much* of a display did he make of her? Was she posed?"

40

Bennet shook her head. "Just abandoned in clear view."

That at least was consistent with the Moonlight Killer. He seemed to take considerable care over the actual murders and the selection of the site, but the aftermath?

Maya looked around again. This might have been the kind of place he would have chosen for a murder: out in the open, well away from anyone else, with the ability to see or hear anyone coming before they could catch up to him.

Was it possible that she was wrong about her theory when it came to the kidnapper? Was it possible that this *was* the Moonlight Killer's work, and she'd accidentally told Harris the truth? *Was* this someone looking for revenge who just hadn't found the Moonlight Killer's real crimes the first couple of times?

No, Maya still wasn't convinced of that. The kidnapper had been able to give Maya a hint on her last case. He'd *known* who the real killer was. If he'd known that, and still sent her, it couldn't be someone hunting the Moonlight Killer; it could only be the Moonlight Killer himself.

Which meant that this case couldn't be him.

"What about the other location?" Maya asked.

"It's an alley a little way from here," Bennet said. "We'll drive over, if you're sure you've seen enough here?"

Maya nodded. She'd wanted to get the general lay of the land, and she'd done that. After a year, there wasn't going to be evidence here waiting to be found.

They left the golf club and drove together. Maya couldn't help noticing Bennet's eyes on her as they did so.

"What is it?" Maya asked.

"I'm just wondering what it takes to get into the FBI."

Was that a note of admiration she heard in the detective's voice?

"I applied right out of the military," Maya said. "The training was hard, but I'm sure it wasn't any worse than what you had to go through at the police academy. Why? Thinking of joining up?"

"Maybe," Bennet said. "I figure if Collingwood and I help catch the Moonlight Killer, we can pretty much write our own ticket rather than... sorry, I'm babbling."

Rather than being stuck in a small city without any action. Maya filled that part in for herself, because it was easy enough to guess. Their boss liked the attention the Moonlight Killer got the department, while

41

they liked the potential the Moonlight Killer had to get attention for them.

The three of them pulled up at the mouth of an alleyway that backed onto a bar. It opened out at either end onto the broader streets of the city. Maya got out and walked it with the other two in tow, looking it over, trying to see how the murder had occurred.

"Jenette Hiatt was returning home from this bar when she was murdered," Collingwood said. "She'd gone out after work; she worked as a sound engineer at a local radio station. She came out after a few drinks, and whoever killed her ambushed her."

"Are there any cameras in the alley?" Maya asked.

"One, watching the rear door of the bar, but it didn't catch any of the attack," Collingwood said. "It didn't catch anyone approaching or leaving, either. There are no cameras that have a view of the mouth of the alley from either end and none near enough that we could work out who went in here from their footage."

Possibly meaning that whoever had done this had scoped out the alley and realized the danger of the camera if he or she struck in the wrong spot.

A more important conclusion sprang into Maya's mind. This definitely wasn't the work of the Moonlight Killer. As far as she knew, the Anne Postmartin case was the only other Moonlight Killer investigation where the body had been moved, and Maya had already proved that wasn't him. He *definitely* wasn't going to kill someone here, then move them all the way to the golf course. The effort that would have taken simply wasn't the way all the files said that he liked to kill.

So who *had* done this?

That was the problem: just looking at the alley and the golf course didn't give Maya any answers. Before, when she'd looked at crime scenes, she'd been able to spot things that other people had missed, been able to get a sense of the way the crime had taken place that had helped to lead her to the killer. Now, there was just a lack of evidence. There was nothing about the layout here that Bennet, Collingwood, and the others had obviously missed.

Maya was going to have to find another way into this case, but what?

"What now?" Bennet asked. She sounded eager, like she was half expecting Maya to have solved all of this already.

"I want to start with the coroner's report," Maya said. "Or better yet, talk to the coroner. After that, I want to speak with Jenette's family."

"That could take time to set up," Collingwood said.

"Then start setting it up now," Maya replied. "If there's one thing I don't have here, it's time."

CHAPTER NINE

Maya didn't spend a lot of time in mortuaries, yet she was standing in one now, watching while the local coroner worked on the autopsy of a young man who seemed to have been hit by a bus.

Maya wasn't squeamish. She'd seen people killed, and worse than killed, when she'd been in the military. She'd seen them mangled by IEDs, torn apart by gunfire. Even so, she had to work hard to keep her composure in the face of everything there.

Bennet was clearly fine with it, although Maya knew enough about body language to know when someone was putting on a mask to keep from showing anything that was underneath. Collingwood wasn't as good at disguising it all yet, so that his disgust was there for several seconds when Maya looked over at him, only turning into the same mask as his colleague with an effort as he saw that she was glancing his way.

The coroner didn't seem to notice any of it. She was a woman in late middle age, wearing a white coat and protective goggles, her dyed blonde hair tied back, her hands covered by blue latex gloves.

"…significant evidence of trauma to the upper left torso…"

"Excuse me," Maya said.

"…Multiple fractures to the pelvis and legs, with limited bruising, suggesting quick blood loss and death…"

On another day, Maya might have waited, but today there wasn't any time. She could feel the time ticking away until the full moon, and she hadn't found anything new at the crime scenes. The golf course had been big and open, easy to spot someone at. The alley had been tight and confined, a good ambush site.

Although, come to think of it, that *did* tell her something: it said that the killer knew what he was doing. He'd planned it and planned it well. It said that there was something deliberate about all this, and that the choices of location *meant* something. Maya needed to work out what, though, and quickly.

"*Excuse* me," Maya repeated, with more emphasis this time.

The coroner looked up. "Yes, Agent?"

"I need to talk to you about the Jenette Hiatt case," Maya said.

"My findings are all in my files, and I have the more recently dead to worry about."

Maya bit back her frustrations. She could even kind of understand why the coroner had said it. She'd worked cold cases long enough to know that they weren't anyone's immediate priority. Ordinarily, that was just a minor frustration, but today, she couldn't wait.

"I was told I would have cooperation here," she said to Bennet and Collingwood. It was a cheap shot, because the two of them had been practically falling over one another to help.

Bennet rushed into action now. "Dr. Eden, the agent is investigating the Moonlight Killer. Chief Strauss has asked us to give the case our top priority."

"I don't work for Chief Strauss," the coroner pointed out.

"I know," Maya said. "And I wouldn't push like this if it weren't urgent, but the FBI has reason to believe that there are still lives at stake here come the full moon."

She saw the surprise on Bennet and Collingwood's faces.

"You think the Moonlight Killer is going to strike again here?" Collingwood blurted out.

That wasn't the way that lives were in danger, but if it got their cooperation, Maya was prepared to let them run with it.

"Dr. Eden…," Bennet began.

"I know, I know," the coroner said. Maya saw her straighten up from her autopsy. "I'm still not sure what you want to know that wouldn't be in my files."

"My hope is that there's something that didn't make it to the file that might prove significant now that more time has passed," Maya said.

Dr. Eden cocked her head to one side. "I put *everything* in my files."

Maya nodded, deliberately. The coroner clearly wasn't someone who was going to welcome disagreement on something like that.

"Even so, can you go through it all with me?"

"Oh, very well," Dr. Eden said. She went over to a tablet and tapped at it a few times. "Jenette Hiatt. Thirty-three years old. Female. Marks on the body suggested strangulation with a ligature, and particles recovered from the body suggest it was something with a rubberized coating. Minor defensive bruising, but not enough to suggest a major fight. Some scrape marks where she was dragged after death."

When the killer moved her from the site of the attack to the golf course.

"Anything to suggest how she was moved?" Maya asked.

Dr. Eden shrugged in response. "There were some contaminants that may have been from a vehicle. If the vehicle in question could be found, I might be able to compare it."

"And the time of death?" Maya asked.

"I'm reasonably certain that it was between nine and ten that night," the coroner said.

"Which fits with when Jenette was seen leaving the bar," Collingwood put in.

Maya nodded. "I want to be clear, the marks on her body suggest that she was moved *after* death? It couldn't be someone who incapacitated her, moved her to the golf course, and then murdered her?"

Maya knew that the Moonlight Killer was more than capable of kidnapping someone before he killed them now, so she wanted to rule out that order of events.

Dr. Eden shook her head, though.

"No, it doesn't fit the lividity. The drag marks were post-mortem."

Meaning a relocation to the golf course.

"And in your professional opinion, is the mode of death consistent with the killings of the Moonlight Killer?" Maya asked.

"Highly consistent," the coroner said, without hesitation. "The ligature method, the lack of major defensive injuries, the clean efficiency of it all, with a complete lack of trace DNA that might be tracked back to the killer. Yes, it's consistent."

"Thank you, doctor," Maya said. "Is there anything else that you were able to discover, or anything that you've thought of since you performed the autopsy?"

Dr. Eden shook her head. "No, I'm sorry, Agent. If you were hoping to get new evidence from me, I'm afraid you've wasted your time."

Maya winced at the thought of the time that was ticking away, but even so, coming here had clarified one or two things for her.

"Thank you, Doctor."

46

She led the way out of the mortuary, and Collingwood, for one, seemed only too happy to get out of there. Bennet seemed a little nonplussed by it all.

"It seems as though you haven't gotten anything new from the crime scenes or from the coroner," she said. Again, she sounded as if she'd half expected Maya to just walk in and spot a solution straight away.

"Sometimes, that's how it goes," Maya said, although she was almost as frustrated. A case where she spotted something new from the start was one where she could quickly find avenues that might lead her to the killer.

"But we're no closer to finding the Moonlight Killer."

That was one area, of course, where she *did* have other avenues to explore, and Maya knew that she couldn't keep this part of it from the detectives forever.

"This isn't the Moonlight Killer."

She could read the surprise on the detectives' faces as clearly as a book.

"Of course it is," Bennet said. "The FBI's serial killer unit came here, and they-"

"The Moonlight Killer doesn't switch sites," Maya said. "He kills his victims in spots where they will be found. He doesn't kill them elsewhere and then drag them somewhere. We've also been doing some work narrowing down his victim profile, and Jenette Hiatt doesn't quite fit it, either."

At least, she wasn't as young as the "bunnies" the Moonlight Killer had taken.

The detectives looked as if they didn't know what to say for several seconds.

"This… this isn't what we expected at all," Bennet said. "I think we're going to have to go and report all of this to Chief Strauss. I don't know if he'll be happy, Agent."

Because having the Moonlight Killer strike in his town meant so much to him. Still, Maya was certain of her findings, and honestly, if this meant that the two detectives wouldn't be following her every step on this, then that probably gave Maya a lot more freedom to act the way she needed to in order to solve this in time.

"That's fine," Maya said. "While you're doing that, I'll keep going with my investigation, and try to find who actually did this. Moonlight Killer or not, there's still a murderer out there in your city."

She saw Bennet nod thoughtfully. "You're right. Of course, you're right. We need to catch whoever this is, even if it's not the Moonlight Killer. But can you *really* be so certain that it's not him, based on a couple of pieces of profiling?"

"I'm sure," Maya said, although she couldn't give away the real reason that she was so sure. So far, only she and Marco Spinelli knew that the kidnapper was the Moonlight Killer, and it was better if it stayed that way, at least for now.

"We should still report all this to the chief," Collingwood said. He didn't look particularly enthusiastic about the prospect. Possibly he'd guessed how his boss might react to the news.

"You go on ahead," Maya said. "I'll make my own way to see Jenette's family, and then meet you back at the precinct afterwards."

The detectives nodded, and then set off towards their car. It gave Maya a little time to think, as she called for a taxi and waited outside the mortuary in the growing warmth of the day.

She hadn't picked up as much new information as she would have liked so far. The perfect scenario would have been if there had been something obvious that the cops had missed thanks to their obsession with the Moonlight Killer, something that pointed straight at someone else and let Maya finish this quickly.

There was nothing like that, but honestly, she hadn't expected it. It was obvious that the Corvallis PD's homicide detectives were competent and thorough. They'd done the legwork on obvious things like chasing down camera footage, and Maya had seen plenty of witness statements in the files, on even small things. She would need to go through all of those.

Yet maybe coming into this with a fresh perspective gave her *some* advantage. For one thing, she wasn't looking in the wrong direction by focusing on the Moonlight Killer, the way the previous investigation had. Maya had seen in her past couple of cases that there was a lot of power in just looking at angles the police hadn't considered before.

Now, she just needed to work out what those angles were.

One thing *was* apparent from the evidence: someone was trying to make this look like the Moonlight Killer deliberately. The parallels to the Moonlight Killer's MO were too clear to be an accident, the way

48

they'd been in her previous case. Someone had decided that they wanted to kill Jenette Hiatt, and they'd realized that the best way to try to get away with it was to deflect the whole investigation into a search for an elusive serial killer.

It meant that this had been planned and planned carefully. This wasn't some crime of passion that had been covered up. This was some deliberately plotted death, coming from a hatred or a grudge that must have been deep and lasting. *That* was the kind of thing that Maya might be able to discover and track to its roots, following the motive until it led back to someone who hated Jenette Hiatt enough to kill her.

To find that person, she needed to start by talking to the people close to Jenette, and she needed to do it quickly, because there wasn't much time before the full moon.

CHAPTER TEN

There was an address for Jenette's sister, Lucinda Hiatt, in the file, so Maya headed over there, and pretty soon found herself standing in front of a brownstone apartment building. She looked over the nameplates and buzzed up, hoping that Jenette's sister would actually be inside.

"Hello?"

"Lucinda Hiatt? This is Agent Gray with the FBI. I was hoping to talk to you about your sister."

"Oh, that's…"

Maya knew she should have called ahead to avoid the feeling that she was just ambushing Jenette's sister, but with so little time to solve the case, she would probably have to do a lot of things in the most direct fashion possible. She'd already used up at least a couple of hours going out to the murder site, and then to the coroner's office.

"May I come up?" Maya asked, pushing the issue.

"Yes, yes of course. 2b."

Maya found herself buzzed through. She went upstairs, to apartment 2b, and found a woman waiting for her who looked remarkably similar to Jenette. She had the same angular features as her sister, but they were softened by a little more weight and by what looked like a deliberate attempt to reduce their impact with dark bangs that flowed down around her face. She gave Maya a worried look as Maya showed her ID.

"I wasn't expecting anyone coming to talk to me after all this time," Lucinda said. She gestured for Maya to come in. The apartment was large and open-plan, but significantly more cluttered than Maya's own place. A large beige sofa dominated the middle of the room, and Lucinda showed her to it before hurrying into the small kitchen space.

"Coffee? I'm not really organized this morning. My boyfriend just went off to work, and I'm on nights this week, so I need all the coffee I can get."

50

"Coffee would be good," Maya said. Right then, she felt as though she probably needed the caffeine even more than Lucinda did. While the other woman made it, Maya cast her eyes around the apartment.

She immediately spotted the pictures of Jenette set out, not just one but close to a dozen, taking up whatever spare surfaces they could.

"You and your sister were close?" Maya asked.

"Very. Do you have any sisters, Agent Gray?"

"I… yes," Maya said.

"Then you know how it can be with them. You grow up always fighting and driving your parents crazy, then one day, you turn around and it turns out that they were your best friend in the world all along."

Maya swallowed at those words, because they reminded her far too much of how things had been with Megan growing up. Her sister had been her best friend and her worst enemy, often over the course of a single day. Now she was trapped, at the mercy of a psychopath.

"Do you know what was going on in her life around the time when she was killed?" Maya asked.

"Why?" Lucinda asked with a frown. "I mean… she was killed by that guy, the Moonlight Killer, right? The police all say so."

Maya considered how much she should say. "I'm looking into alternative possibilities, just in case anything was missed in the first investigation."

"Yes, but it wasn't, was it?" Lucinda said. She came over with coffee. "It was him; I know it."

"I still have to go through everything," Maya said. She understood that it might be easier in some ways for Lucinda to believe that her sister had been killed by a serial killer. The Moonlight Killer might be evil and unfathomable, but in a way that still made more sense than believing that someone close to Jenette, someone Lucinda might know, was the killer.

"How will going through my sister's life help to catch him, though?" Lucinda asked.

Maya knew that if she kept pushing at the idea that it definitely wasn't the Moonlight Killer, she risked pushing Jenette's sister away, so that she wouldn't help at all. It felt wrong to go along with the idea, but if it got to the truth, then maybe it was for the greater good.

"If it is the Moonlight Killer," Maya said, "then knowing more about Jenette's life might tell me how and when he started to target her.

If it isn't, then it might help me to find anyone else who wanted to hurt her. Either way, I'm going to do my best to get to the truth of all this."

Lucinda took a sip of her coffee. "I guess so. I mean, what do you want to know?"

"Let's start with Jenette's routines," Maya said. "Did she do things the same way every day?"

"Pretty much," Lucinda said. "She would get up, go to the gym or go running, head off to work at the local radio station, then usually go out after work to a bar or something. She liked to party. She was pretty popular."

A consistent routine might make it easier to spot anything that deviated from that around the time she was killed.

"And was there anything different near the time when she was killed?" Maya asked.

Lucinda shook her head. "Not that I saw."

"Was there anyone who *didn't* like her?" Maya asked. "Did she have any enemies? Any rivals at work, any exes with a grudge, anyone at all who might have any reason to want to hurt her?"

"Well…," For a moment or two, Maya thought that Lucinda might just shake her head and go back to insisting that it had to be the Moonlight Killer. "I suppose there was Ray."

"Who's Ray?" Maya asked.

"One of her ex-boyfriends, from a while back. Not even that, really. It was kind of a casual thing for her, but he didn't see it that way. He ended up showing up outside her work, coming around to her place… she had to get a restraining order to stop him."

A restraining order? Just the sound of it made hope jump in Maya's chest, because if this guy was obsessed enough to stalk Jenette, it was possible that he was obsessed enough to do more. Not all stalkers escalated, but enough did that Maya knew that she suddenly had an avenue to explore.

"What's his full name?" Maya asked.

"Ray Heartford. I don't want to get him into trouble though; I'm sure he would never do anything like this. Only someone… well, someone like a serial killer would do something like this."

Maya wished that were true. As it was, though, she at least had a place to start looking.

*

52

Maya wasn't entirely surprised to find Chief Strauss waiting for her when she got back to the local precinct.

"What's this I hear about you thinking that this isn't the Moonlight Killer?" he said, not even bothering with the usual pleasantries. Had Maya managed to sour things here so easily, just by not going along with the prevailing wisdom on the case?

"I just need to look into every possibility," Maya said. "And this case doesn't fit the most typical pattern."

"The strangulation of a woman with a ligature on the night of the full moon?" Chief Strauss countered. "I know you have a job to do, Agent Gray, but you're wasting your time looking for anything else."

"Then I waste my time," Maya said, as if wasting time in all of this weren't the biggest fear she had. Already, she'd used up a lot of her first day in Corvallis. By the time she was done looking into Ray Heartford, how much would be left?

"If the FBI isn't taking this seriously-"

"Trust me, Chief Strauss, I am taking this more seriously than you can imagine."

Something of the desperation Maya felt around the case, the need to get her sister back, must have come out in her voice, because Chief Strauss fell quiet for a moment or two.

"Look at it this way," Maya said. "If I look into other possibilities and conclude that it has to have been the Moonlight Killer, there's that much more certainty about it. If I find another killer... well, it's a murder solved without having to throw the full resources of your department at it."

"True enough," Chief Strauss conceded. Maya could tell that he still wasn't entirely sold on it, but at least he wasn't actively trying to stop her. "I've set aside an office for you to use, with computer access to our network for any files you need. It's just through here."

The office was basic, but more than enough for Maya's needs, with a computer station on a desk, a chair, and a board to use as an evidence board if she needed.

"Thank you," Maya said. "Will Bennet and Collingwood-"

"If you need them to hunt for the Moonlight Killer, just ask," Chief Strauss said. The implication was clear: if she *wasn't* hunting for the serial killer, she could do it alone.

"That's fine," Maya said. She waited for Chief Strauss to leave the office, and then started to look Jenette Hiatt up online.

There were the usual news articles and tributes, of course. Maya looked past those. She was more interested in the real woman, and if she'd made any more enemies who had been overlooked in the search for the Moonlight Killer.

Maya found a couple of mentions of her on an archived copy of a radio station's website, under their staff pages. Jenette was there smiling out in a picture of her at a mixing desk.

Jenette has been with CDR for three years, working on a wide variety of different shows. One of the most popular members of our team, when she isn't mixing your favorite radio station, she can be found doing triathlons or enjoying Corvallis's nightlife.

It was the standard kind of thing people put when they had to provide a bio for themselves on a company site. It didn't tell Maya much except that Jenette had been careful to make herself look good there.

Perhaps her social media would tell Maya more.

Maya started to look for it, but quickly found that there wasn't much there to find. Where a lot of people's accounts lingered ghost-like after they were gone, Jenette's mostly seemed to have been taken down. Maybe her sister had done it, or some conscientious colleague? Wasn't appointing someone to deal with taking down your social media as much a thing these days as asking them to deal with your stuff, or look after your pets?

It meant that there was frustratingly little to find. Except that it occurred to Maya that sometimes, people weren't as thorough about that kind of thing as they hoped. She kept trawling until she came up with a messaging account that seemed to be in Jenette's name. She fired off a quick email to some of the tech people back at the FBI headquarters, then waited.

It wasn't long before the account opened up to her like a flower, letting Maya see the last message threads there before Jenette's death. The most recent ones were likely to be the ones she needed, but even so, Maya read through everything she could get.

Even the briefest glance showed that Jenette wasn't quite the saint that her sister and the corporate website wanted to portray her as.

Just fill in for me, Suzi, or I'll tell K that you're the one who blew up his story on the lake before he could finish it.

Why are you even working at the station, when you mix that badly?

Is it just me, or does Wendy look like she's had work done?

In every message stream Maya saw the sharper side of Jenette. She was, quite frankly, a bully.

Then Maya saw one between her and Ray Heartford.

You're a useless, spineless man. You want to know why I stopped seeing you? Because you never had the guts to do *anything. Why don't you just throw yourself off a bridge, or something, and make the world a better place? Oh, and I'm telling that new girlfriend of yours every secret you thought you managed to hide from me.*

Even compared to the rest of it, the tone was nasty. The kind of thing that might get a reaction. The kind of thing, just maybe, that might push someone who already hated her to do more. In that moment, Maya knew that she had to speak to Ray Heartford.

CHAPTER ELEVEN

Even though it was getting into evening, Maya hurried to her rental car, knowing that she had to talk to Ray Heartford right now, today. He was her most plausible lead, and she couldn't let this go for the night.

A quick look through the electronic files for the case gave Maya an address for Ray Heartford. Apparently, he worked from home, doing something in marketing, so there was no reason that he shouldn't be there. Maya had no compunctions about just showing up at his door. If anything, it was probably better to catch him off guard, to see if he would let anything slip that he otherwise might try to hold back.

Maya pulled up outside the house, making sure that she was ready for this. Ray had been a stalker and might be a murderer. She'd had suspects turn violent the moment they thought they were being found out before. Whatever happened, though, Maya was sure that she would be ready for it.

The house was small and suburban, surrounded by a strip of lawn, with couple of cars on the driveway. Ray wasn't there alone, then. The files said nothing about who might be there with him; but then, why would they?

As Maya ran through them again on her tablet, they *did* offer one piece of information that made Maya pause. The original investigation had talked to him, but dismissed him as a suspect, citing a potential alibi. Maya read through that section more closely.

"A bar receipt?" Maya said in surprise as she read through it. "That's his whole alibi?"

According to the file, Ray had a receipt for a bar twenty minutes away from around the time of the murder. Yet Maya could see all kinds of problems with that as an alibi: the coroner had given an hour window for Jenette's death, giving Ray more than enough time to slip out if he wanted, get over to where she was, and kill her. He could even have done things the other way around, if he'd been willing to leave a body in the trunk of his car while he sat in a bar to establish an alibi.

Maya found herself staring at the cars on the driveway. One was a large sedan, with a trunk more than big enough to put a body in.

Maya strode up to the door, hit the doorbell, and got her ID ready. It was answered by a woman of about thirty, plump and round faced, with auburn hair and green eyes.

"Hello?" the woman said. "Can I help you?"

"I'm Agent Gray with the FBI," Maya said. "I'm looking for Ray Heartford. I'm reinvestigating the death of Jenette Hiatt."

"Her?" the woman said. She didn't sound happy about it. "Of course, it would be her. Ray! There's a woman here from the FBI who wants to talk to you."

A man came to the door beside her. He was ordinary looking, slightly out of shape, with spiked dark hair and glasses.

"This is about Jenette, isn't it?"

Maya nodded. "I need to talk to you about her."

Maya could see how uncomfortable he was about that prospect. Was that just that he was sick of dealing with something like this, or was he trying to hide something?

"You'd better come in," Ray said. "This is my fiancé, Chloe."

The house was filled with memorabilia that seemed to be related to different bands and radio stations. There were more posters on the walls than blank spaces, while shelves held figurines, replica gold disks, and more.

Ray led the way through to a living room where a couple of pizza boxes were open on a small coffee table. It seemed that was what dinner looked like here. Maya took a seat on the edge of one of a couple of armchairs. She didn't settle back into it completely, just in case she had to get up and run after Ray. He didn't *look* like a runner, but it was impossible to be sure.

He and Chloe sat together on a couch, holding hands. Maya caught their nervous glances across to one another.

"Do you want to do this with Chloe here?" Maya asked. It was possible that she didn't know about the stalking. If so, and it somehow turned out that Ray hadn't been involved in this, she didn't want to ruin their relationship.

Then again, she probably had a right to know.

"There's nothing you can say that I don't already know, Agent," Chloe said.

"Really? So you know that he stalked and harassed Jenette Hiatt in the months before her death?"

"It wasn't like that," Ray said, the discomfort in the protestation obvious.

Maya cocked her head to one side. "So what was it like? Jenette got a restraining order against you."

"Ok, so I tried to cling onto our relationship," Ray said. "But the restraining order… it was just one more way for her to hurt me."

Maya frowned. She wasn't sure if she believed that or not. She knew stalkers tended to have a fairly twisted view of what was really happening. One in which they thought their victims either deserved the harassment, or worse, actually *wanted* it. Even so, the best way to get answers here was to listen.

"What do you mean by that?" Maya asked.

"He means that Jenette was a bully," Chloe put in. "And that she put the restraining order in place as a way to remind Ray that she was the one with all the power, even after their relationship."

"So your relationship wasn't a good one?" Maya asked Ray.

She saw him shake his head. "She was like this drug I couldn't get enough of, but she was terrible for me. She used to say the cruelest things to me; she seemed as though she got off on hurting me. Then when she got bored with me, she broke things off like I was nothing; and yes, I shouldn't have stuck around then, but she made a game out of that, too, like she wanted to know she could snap her fingers and have me back, but didn't actually want me. When I got frustrated with all that, she made out that I was some kind of stalker, and had a restraining order slapped on me."

Again, Maya was all too aware of the ways that stalkers could twist the facts in their own minds to make their behaviors seem reasonable to themselves, yet something about the things Ray was saying fit with what Maya had seen of Jenette in her messages. She clearly liked to play games with people, and she was cruel almost for the sake of it.

Of course, that didn't take away Ray's motive for murder. Quite the opposite, if anything. It just confirmed how much he might want to get rid of the woman who was making his life a living hell, once and for all.

Maya didn't want to just come out and accuse him yet, though. She needed to work up to this and see what his feelings really were.

"You must have been pretty angry about her treating you like that," Maya said.

"I was," Ray admitted. "That was part of why I was still hanging around her. And maybe I said some things I shouldn't have, too."

"I've seen all the messages that went between the two of you," Maya said, watching to see how Ray would react.

He paled for a second or two. He obviously knew how bad some of it looked.

"Look, I'm sorry for how I was in some of it. I should have handled things better. But if you've seen the messages, then you also saw what she was like. Getting out of that relationship proved to be the best thing that could have happened to me. If I'd still been stuck chasing after Jenette, I would never have found Chloe, and we wouldn't be engaged now."

"Congratulations," Maya said. "Although you know I have to ask... exactly when did your relationship with Chloe start?"

"Pretty much immediately after he broke up with that bitch," Chloe supplied. "I got to see what she was like firsthand. I'm sorry she's dead, obviously, but, if it had to be anyone..."

It occurred to Maya that there might be more than one person in this relationship with a reason to make sure that Jenette Hiatt stayed out of the picture.

"Isn't this all pretty academic anyway?" Chloe asked. "Everyone knows that the Moonlight Killer did it. It's just about the only interesting thing to ever happen here."

"Interesting?" Maya said. "That's not the word I'd choose."

Although it seemed to be the way plenty of the town, including the police department, saw things.

"Chloe's a fan of true crime," Ray said, as if that made it all ok. It explained things, at least, but it also caught Maya's interest.

Presumably, Chloe would have read about the Moonlight Killer at some point. There were certainly enough books out there, putting out different theories. She would have the knowledge needed to copy the crimes and get the details right.

"I still have to ask where you were on the night of the murder," Maya said, looking over at Ray.

"I told the cops, I was in a bar. I even showed them the receipt."

"You did," Maya agreed, "but how long would it really take you to get from that bar to the one Jenette was killed outside? Do you have anything else that shows you were there the whole time?"

"What? You really think I might have done this?" Ray said.

"I don't know," Maya said. "I have to ask, though. I'm afraid I have to ask you the same question, Chloe."

"*Me?*" Chloe said.

Maya nodded, taking in the surprise. Maybe that meant that she'd had nothing to do with any of this, or maybe it just meant that she hadn't been expecting anyone to ever lock her way over this.

"If you were seeing Ray at the time, then it's reasonable to think that you might have acted to protect him from someone you saw as dangerous to your relationship," Maya said. "So I need to know where you were that night."

For a moment or two, Maya thought that they might not answer, and if they didn't, she would have a difficult choice to make. Did she bring them in and hope that one or the other of them cracked when interrogated, or did she leave them and try to find some physical evidence first? In a live case, it would have been the second option every time; but in a cold case, there often simply wasn't any new physical evidence to find.

Then Ray looked over to Chloe and smiled.

"That bar I was at? We were both there. We had dinner. It was one of our earliest dates. It seems I have yet another reason to be grateful that I found her."

"Does that answer your questions, Agent?" Chloe said, and there was a firmness in her tone that made it clear that the two of them weren't going to be adding anything more.

Maya nodded, hiding the frustration she felt. She'd come there in the hope that the answer to this might be as simple as an alibi that wouldn't hold up under any kind of pressure. Now, Ray had an alibi that would be almost impossible to disprove without finding new evidence. More than that, it was an alibi that Maya believed. Neither he nor his fiancé was the killer Maya was looking for. Whoever *that* was, they were still out there.

Maya had to find them, but she'd already used up almost an entire day, and she wasn't any closer. If she didn't think of something soon, the full moon was going to come around, and two women, not one, would die.

CHAPTER TWELVE

Through his headphones, the world spread out around him. He sat outside his target's apartment, listening to the sounds of her moving around it, listening to the friends who had come around unexpectedly for dinner.

It was one reason he wouldn't act here. Too many people. Too much chance of being disturbed.

He heard the sizzle of a skillet, the softer sound of the flame beneath it. Sound couldn't give him the ingredients, but the cameras in the apartment caught the three of them. A young man, a woman the same age, and his target.

"It's so good to get to entertain for once. I don't get to do this enough with work. I'm on the same shift pattern all week."

As he listened in, he made notes, tracking any information that might prove useful. There was little that was new now, though. He'd gotten to know her very well by this point. Probably, he could predict every move she would ever make.

The last thing he wanted to do now was sit and listen to her enjoying herself like this. He didn't want her to be happy. He wanted her to suffer and die, the way she deserved to. The way she *had* to, after all the trouble he had gone to.

Instead of continuing to listen to the apartment, he drove off, picking a new spot and just listening to the sounds of the city around him. If his target left her apartment or made a call, he would know, anyway.

Instead, he tuned into the different streams floating around the city, pulling them in, filtering them, listening, learning. It was amazing what people left out there unguarded, or as close to it as made no difference. The lack of security some people showed was as good as an invitation to listen to their lives.

He could have picked any of them for this, but they hadn't done all that she had done. They didn't deserve this the way that she did.

He sat and listened to a couple argue, then to a group of teens in a park, discussing a drug deal so minor it barely even counted as one.

When it amused him to, he tapped into the local CCTV cameras to put faces to the voices that came through shotgun microphones and intercepted signals, but for the most part it was easier to just let the sound wash over himself through the headphones.

After a while, he turned his attention to the police. They had been a little harder to listen in on than his target, but not by much. Honestly, it had been almost too easy to get to the point where he could listen to everything they said over their radios and their phone systems.

Knowing them was almost as important as knowing his victim. He jotted down every patrol route, every pattern he could find in when they went off shift to eat or changed over personnel. Already, he could start to see the gaps he could exploit.

"...do you make of the new woman? The FBI agent?"

He caught those words over one of the police channels using his scanner, and focused his attention through his headphones, wanting to hear what that was about.

"I'm not sure. I thought she'd come here to find the Moonlight Killer. I think everyone did. Now, it's like she doesn't even think it was him. Today, she was looking at Jenette Hiatt's personal life, like the answer is going to be *there*. Like we didn't check."

They had checked. He could remember them checking. He'd listened to every word of their original investigation. At first, he'd assumed that he would have to run if they got too close, that he would hear them coming for him and flee. Then, gradually, it had become clear just how well his little deception with the style of the Moonlight Killer had worked. They'd bought it absolutely, and he'd been free to keep going with his work.

"She'll give up soon enough," one of the cops said.

"I'm not so sure about that. I met her. There's something determined about her, like there's something personal about this. She's not going to give up."

"Then maybe Agent Gray will find the Moonlight Killer for us, and we can be the town that *caught* him."

Agent Gray. A name drifting out over the airwaves. Just a small slip, but definitely something to look into. If the FBI were in town, and they weren't going along with his little misdirection as neatly as last time, then he needed to know everything there was to know about this "Agent Gray."

Would this mess with his plans? Briefly, a thin thread of panic spread through him. The cops had said that she was looking elsewhere to try to find Jenette Hiatt's killer, so what if she looked *his* way. It wasn't as if he could just erase his connection to her, or the reasons that she had needed to die.

"You really think she'll find anything?" one of the cops asked.

"They say she's the best, when it comes to cold cases," the other replied. "They say she found out that some cops in Louisiana had arrested the wrong guy in less than a day."

His worries started to spread further. If Agent Gray really was that good, maybe she was even up to the task of finding him, in spite of all the precautions he took. Maybe he should bring his plans forward.

No. He needed to calm down. He had planned this meticulously. There was no reason to suspect that anyone knew about him yet, or that they would find anything out at all. It was better to stick to the plan he'd prepared, the one that all this surveillance had been building towards.

In two days, his target would die. In the meantime, though, he would keep a close eye on Agent Gray, so that she didn't get too close to the truth without him knowing.

CHAPTER THIRTEEN

Maya fell asleep in a cheap hotel room in Corvallis, still going through Jenette Hiatt's messaging feeds. She didn't intend to, it was just that one minute she was going through another round of bile and bullying from the murder victim, and the next, she found herself waking up to morning sunlight, still in her clothes.

Maya groaned and stretched uncomfortably. This wasn't the way she'd planned on things going. By now, she should have had some kind of lead in the case, should have had *some* clue about which direction to go in next.

Getting coffee, she started up her laptop, and found herself imagining what Marco would say if he were there. Probably that she shouldn't even touch it until she'd had breakfast and taken a shower. Probably that looking after herself counted for as much as the case.

Maya wasn't sure that she believed that, though, not when there were lives on the line.

She started to look through the messages again, just in case there was something she had missed.

Mess with me again, and I'll make sure that all your shows come out sounding like they were recorded on a wax cylinder.

All I'm saying is that Jess has been talking about you behind your back.

The problem with the messages was simple: Jenette Hiatt had been a bully to just about everyone. Her sister might think that she was wonderful, but even she had conceded that they'd spent plenty of time arguing. Maya wasn't sure that she counted as the most impartial of character witnesses.

Jenette had been cruel to so many people, it was impossible to work out which of them might have wanted to kill her. There were no obvious signs online, no one who stood out from the rest. No one had made threats towards her, and Maya suspected that if they had, the Corvallis police department would have found them.

With a sigh, Maya closed her laptop and set off for the precinct. She needed to start this again. She needed to go through all the possible suspects, and to do that, she needed help.

Maya's phone pinged with a message. A glance at it told her that it was from Marco.

Hope things are going ok over there. I know I can't be there but let me know if you need anything. I was worried the other night.

Maya ignored the message for now. She needed to focus, and it was hard to focus on anything other than Marco when he was involved.

She arrived at the station, rushed up to the second floor, and hurried to the office that they'd given her. Maya was quite surprised to find Collingwood and Bennet there, given what Chief Strauss had said to her yesterday.

"Here to get me back on track, looking for the Moonlight Killer?" Maya asked.

Bennet shrugged. "If it's him, we're going to help you find him."

"And if it's not?" Maya said.

"Then we help anyway," Collingwood said.

It seemed that Strauss had undergone a change of heart overnight. Maya wasn't sure if she fully believed it, and she half suspected that the two detectives were there just to watch her, but right then, she would take all the help she could get.

"I need someone to go through the people who Jenette Hiatt argued with online," Maya said.

She opened up her laptop and pulled up the messaging account to show the others.

"That's a lot of messages," Collingwood said.

"It's also something we've seen before," Bennet added, looking over the contents. "We went through this at the time of the murder, but no one stood out as making threats or being a particular target, aside from her ex. He had an alibi."

"I know." Maya knew exactly how strong that alibi was now. "But there's going through this and then there's looking into each of the people here. When you looked at the messages, did you check if each of them had any reason beyond this to hurt her? Did you get statements from each of them?"

"Not once the Moonlight Killer angle came up," Bennet admitted.

"Then that's what I want," Maya said. "Call them. Ask them. Specifically, ask them about each other. Find out if there was anyone who had more of a reason than the rest to dislike Jenette."

"That will take all day," Bennet said.

Maya nodded. "I know, but it still needs to be done."

It was also why *she* wasn't doing it. With only today and tomorrow before the full moon, there wasn't enough time for Maya to track down everyone Jenette had bullied online. She could leave that to the detectives, though, while she tried to work through other avenues of inquiry.

"What are you going to be doing while I do all this?" Bennet asked.

"I've spoken to her sister, I've spoken to her ex. Now I want to look at her finances and legal affairs, to see if anything stands out there. I take it you pulled those aspects on the original case?"

Collingwood nodded. "The files are hardcopy, though, to preserve confidentiality."

"I need to see them."

Collingwood gestured to the door, and Maya followed him out, through the station, to an elevator. They took it down to a basement level, where Maya caught the scent of mildew and old paper.

"The archives are just through here," Collingwood said.

He punched in a key code on a door and led her through to a space where row after row of filing cabinets sat like some bureaucratic army waiting for orders. The information Maya needed would be in there somewhere, but it was a question of finding it.

"I'll dig out the file for you." Collingwood said.

Maya would say this for him and Bennet: even if they didn't believe that she was going the right way on this, they were still being more than helpful about it. This wasn't like Louisiana, where she'd had to fight her way through harassment from the local cops on top of the case itself. It wasn't even like Cleveland, where Marco had been the only one to go along with her thinking that it wasn't the Moonlight Killer.

Thoughts of Marco made Maya check her phone again. There were more messages there from him, but she didn't read them. A string of messages like that felt more like the kind of thing a partner or boyfriend might have sent, and Maya didn't have enough time to think about him like that right then.

There was another reason she didn't look: she didn't want Marco telling her how worried he was again. Maya knew as well as anyone that she should slow down, that she should take some space to breathe, but there *wasn't* any space. If Maya hesitated now, then it might cost her sister her life.

"Here we go," Collingwood said, bringing out a thicker version of the case file. They took it over to a table and started to look through it. Collingwood leaned in as Maya looked it over, obviously trying to spot anything, possibly trying to impress her.

Was he trying to impress her? Maya looked over at him, and she could see the eagerness there on his face. Was that just because she was an FBI agent and he wanted to show her that he could do the job as well as she could? Or was it something more than that?

"You must have worked some impressive cases," Collingwood said, as Maya tried to work through Jenette's financial records.

"I work cold cases," Maya said. "It's not as though I'm out hunting down terrorists."

"Cold cases are impressive enough," Collingwood said. "You come in after everyone else has decided that there's nothing else to find, and you find it anyway."

"Sometimes," Maya said.

"More than that. I heard you found two murderers in the last two weeks. And that even before that, you'd solved dozens of cases."

"Where did you hear that?" Maya asked.

She saw Collingwood shrug. "I have my sources. We're not all small-town rubes out here, you know."

"I never thought anyone here was," Maya said.

He was trying as hard to be helpful as Marco had, back in Cleveland, but Maya didn't feel anything like the same way she had with him.

"Do you see any unusual transactions, anything that shouldn't be there?" Collingwood asked. It was the right question, but right then, it was a distraction.

"Nothing so far," Maya said. "But I need to look closer."

Maya worked through it, looking at Jenette's accounts. As far as she could see, there were no unusual transactions. No large amounts of money came in beyond her salary from the radio station. None went out that weren't obviously the rent on her apartment or regular bills.

Maya wasn't sure quite *what* she was looking for. Something that might point to blackmail, maybe, or to a side to Jenette's life that wasn't out in the open. Something that might show where someone had taken money from her, either before or after her death. Any one of those might push someone towards murder.

There wasn't anything, though. Nothing stood out, nothing seemed strange. All the transactions were the same from month to month, and all of them seemed easy to identify as the normal kinds of things anyone might spend money on: rent, gym membership, groceries, restaurants.

"I still don't really get why you're so certain that this isn't the Moonlight Killer," Collingwood said after a while.

"Why are *you* so certain that it was?" Maya snapped back, because she still couldn't go into all the details of how she knew that the Moonlight Killer wasn't behind this. She also couldn't lead Collingwood through this by the nose. She had a job to do and not enough time to do it in.

"The rest of the FBI seemed pretty sure when they were here," Collingwood said. "They took one look at us, and decided it was obviously him. Not like the one over in Albany."

Maya turned to point out that the FBI had obviously changed their mind, given that she was here, but froze halfway as Collingwood's words started to sink in.

"What 'one over in Albany?'" Maya demanded. Did Collingwood mean what she thought he meant?

"There was a woman killed about six months back, on the night of the full moon. A doctor. But the FBI never went over there. They never decided that her killing had anything to do with the Moonlight Killer."

"Why haven't I heard about this?" Maya demanded, unable to keep the sharpness out of her voice. "Why did nobody tell me about this before now?"

"Don't blame me," Collingwood said. "I didn't know that you'd want to know about some completely separate crime."

Was that really what it was in his head? Because the FBI hadn't made the connection, he was happy to ignore the obvious similarities of the MO and the timing?

Why hadn't Maya heard about it before? The answer to that was obvious: it was a local crime that had never been flagged as a potential Moonlight Killer murder. For some reason, no one at the local level had

68

ever sent it up the line, and no one had picked it up in the FBI's dedicated task force.

Because it hadn't been picked up, it wasn't in the files Maya had gone through.

"How was she killed?" Maya asked.

"I don't know," Collingwood said. "It was Albany's case, not ours."

Maya knew then that she needed to be in Albany. If there was another crime out there so similar in its timing, there was a good chance that it was linked. If it was, then that link might provide Maya with the evidence she needed to get to the bottom of all of this.

Turning, she ran for the door to the archives. She needed to get to Albany, and she didn't have any time to waste.

CHAPTER FOURTEEN

Maya drove over to Albany, still not able to believe that a second murder with such a similar MO had somehow not been mentioned to her until now.

That it wasn't in the files was bad enough, but at least understandable: the murders in the FBI's Moonlight Killer files only made it there because they had been reported as such, flagged up by local cops as possibilities. The fact that Maya had spent a day investigating all of this, and she had only learned about this second murder because of a passing comment by Collingwood? That made her wonder if this batch of local police understood how their job was meant to work.

Albany came into view. It was about the same size as Corvallis, which was to say it was a small city, without the looming high rises of somewhere like D.C. Maya could see a couple of industrial areas, but again, it seemed to be a place that traded on the prettiness of the surrounding landscape as much as on what it produced. There were so many trees in among the houses that driving up to it, it was almost possible to believe that someone had just built a town in the middle of a forest without bothering to clear any of the surrounding vegetation. The effect was to hide a lot of the town's suburbs, so that Maya barely noticed the transition as she started to drive through them.

She headed for the Linn County Sheriff's department, only flinching slightly at the thought of another sheriff after her run-ins with Sheriff Recks in Louisiana. The building was squat and solid looking, set in the heart of the city. Maya went in, into a broad, open reception area where a young deputy seemed to be looking over things from a desk. He was muscled like a football player, with the beginnings of a beard.

Maya showed him her badge. "I'm Agent Gray, with the FBI cold cases unit. I need to speak to the sheriff."

"You're talking to him. Sheriff O'Neil, at your service."

That caught Maya a little by surprise. She'd assumed that this was a deputy, just because he was so young.

"Sorry, I thought…"

"I get that a lot," Sheriff O'Neil said. "What brings you to Albany, Agent Gray?"

He seemed friendly enough, but there was a note of wariness there.

"I'm told that there was a murder here about six months ago, on the night of the full moon."

Maya saw the wariness in the sheriff's expression increase.

"You here chasing the Moonlight Killer, Agent?" he said. "They tell you all about how he struck there in Corvallis but not here?"

Maya had the sense of some rivalry that she didn't want to get caught up in. Even so, she knew that she had to ask questions.

"I was in Corvallis, re-investigating the murder of Jenette Hiatt. One of the police there mentioned that there was a similar killing here, and I was hoping that exploring any connections between them might lead to whoever did this."

"Whoever did this?" Sheriff O'Neil said.

Maya decided that the best thing to do was to just come out and say it, especially since Sheriff O'Neil seemed to be so wary of the idea of the Moonlight Killer.

"I don't think that the Moonlight Killer murdered Jenette Hiatt. I think that someone was trying to copy his methods and his timing in order to disguise his crimes. The woman who was murdered here…"

"Cynthia Yoo."

"I think there's a chance that she was murdered by the same person, and if there *is* a link, then there might be a chance that looking into the crimes side by side might tell us more."

The sheriff stood there for a moment or two, blinking at her. "You're *really* not here chasing the Moonlight Killer?"

Maya shook her head. "As far as I know, he's never struck two places so close together, but waited six months between the killings. He likes to spread out his murders. But I think there *is* a killer who has killed both here and in Corvallis. Can I take a look at your files on this one?"

After her experiences elsewhere, Maya half expected Sheriff O'Neil to tell her no, to have to fight just to get the basics on the case. Instead, though, he nodded.

"Of course. Come through."

He led the way through to an office where there were a couple of deputies working at desks, and several filing cabinets along the back

71

wall. Sheriff O'Neil went to one of them and pulled out a file, setting it down in front of Maya.

"Cynthia Yoo, thirty-five," he said, giving Maya the details even before she opened the file. "Killed on the night of the full moon by strangulation. Found down near the river, in a spot that's popular with anglers."

"A display site," Maya said, and saw the sheriff nod.

"A local runner caught a glimpse of the man who dumped the body," Sheriff O'Neil said, and Maya felt her excitement spike.

"They did?" This could be the break she was looking for in this case. "Were you able to get a description? Anything at all might give me something to go on when I compare the cases."

"Don't get your hopes up," Sheriff O'Neil said. "The most we got was general shape, quite large, quite bulky, and they were fairly sure it was a man. Beyond that, nothing, because they were wrapped up in a jacket, hat, and scarf. The runner says that they shouted, but the guy didn't even look around. Then when he got closer, the guy spotted him and ran for it. The runner thought about chasing after him but thought better of it."

That was probably just as well, as far as Maya was concerned. Most people overestimated how well they could deal with dangerous situations. If the runner had given chase, there might have been two murders in Albany, not one.

Maya started to flick through the file, looking at the autopsy photographs. They looked remarkably similar to Jenette Hiatt's.

"Tell me about Cynthia," she said.

"She was a doctor, an ENT specialist, focusing on hearing loss."

An interesting job, but one that seemed very different from Jenette Hiatt's, with no connection to the entertainment industry. Their looks were quite different, too. Where Jenette had been angular and sharp edged, the photographs of Cynthia showed an Asian American woman with round features. They had both been women of about the same age, but beyond that, Maya couldn't see a connection that would attract a serial killer to both of them.

Maya stopped as she registered that thought. A serial killer? Was she sure that was what this was? At this stage, it was too early to say.

"She was recently divorced, and it was messy, but we eliminated the husband as a suspect," Sheriff O'Neil said. "He was with his new girlfriend that night, all night. We had to look at other angles."

72

Maya nodded. It sounded as though the sheriff had done the work there correctly. She didn't want to go over that ground again.

"So if the river was the dump site, do you have the actual location of the murder?" Maya asked.

Sheriff O'Neil nodded. "We managed to narrow it down with forensics, and by tracking Cynthia's movements. Would you like me to show you?"

Maya nodded.

"Yes please."

*

The place the sheriff showed her was a small back lot, with garages on either side, overshadowed by the buildings around it. There were no cars parked there, and from here, it wasn't possible to be seen from the surrounding streets. There were also multiple avenues of escape, with two or three small alleys leading off.

It struck Maya as the perfect spot in which to stage an ambush.

"He killed Cynthia here?" Maya said, wanting to be certain about it.

She saw Sheriff O'Neil nod. "We think she went through this alley on her way to meet with a friend in a restaurant over that way. Either she walked through it, and he attacked her, or he was waiting at the mouth of the alley and grabbed her as she walked past."

Maya looked over at the alley the sheriff pointed to. A walk along it confirmed that it opened out onto a bright, tree lined street. Exactly the kind of space that someone might feel comfortable walking along. Cynthia had probably felt certain that she was safe, right up until the moment when someone attacked her.

What then? Maya could imagine how it might have gone all too easily. There would have been the initial few seconds of panic as he grabbed her, because without training, people almost always panicked when someone attacked them. Probably, the attacker would have gotten the ligature around her neck in those seconds, trying to make sure that she didn't cry out.

After that, he'd dragged her back into the alley. That suggested some degree of strength, consistent with the large, bulky figure the jogger had seen later. Maya could imagine how terrified Cynthia would have been in the moments before she died, her hands scrabbling at the rope that strangled her. He'd killed her here and then... what? Did he have a vehicle waiting to take her down to the river? He must have done it, to avoid being spotted.

"I take it there are no cameras near here?" Maya said.

Sheriff O'Neil shook his head again. "It's a blind spot. We tried checking cameras further out, but once you get more than a little way from the site, it becomes impossible to work out whether a vehicle was heading here or somewhere else."

Again, that pointed to something well planned. The murderer had picked this spot for a reason. He'd worked out that he could make a kill here without being seen and executed his plan with ruthless efficiency.

The fact that he'd moved Cynthia and Jenette after he'd killed them was interesting. Was that just about making sure the bodies were found after the full moon, so that the Moonlight Killer would be blamed? Maya guessed that it was, but she also found herself wondering why he'd killed both of his targets before moving them. Wouldn't it have been easier for him to hold a gun on them and force them to go to the place he wanted them found, *then* kill them? She found herself wondering if he'd done it this way because he wanted to avoid any chance of his victims escaping, or if it was something else.

If so, though, what?

"The big question is if this was random, or if there was some kind of bigger point to it," Maya said. She could see the worry on the sheriff's face at that.

"Are you saying that we might have someone out here who kills women at random?"

Maya hoped not, because that would make this case almost impossible to crack. It was only too easy, though, to imagine a killer picking a site like this and then just waiting, watching until a suitable target came by like an alligator waiting just below the surface of a lake.

"I don't know what to think at the moment," Maya said. "Did Jenette Hiatt's name come up at all in your investigation into this case? Even peripherally?"

Sheriff O'Neil stood there for a moment. "I don't think so. I'll check more when I get back to the station."

"Thank you," Maya said. She had to hope for some kind of connection beyond merely a shared killer, because that was a thread she could unravel, trying to find a way back to the man who'd done this. If it was random, then there was nothing to go on, and more women would die.

74

"What are you going to do in the meantime?" Sheriff O'Neil asked. "You heading back to the Corvallis PD?"

Even now, Maya could hear the slight note of dislike there as he mentioned the other city's police department. That rivalry had stopped either side from noticing the connection between these cases. It meant that a killer was still out there who might have been caught by now.

"I'm going to look into Cynthia more, and see if I can find any link, anything that might point me in the right direction. You said she was an ENT specialist?"

"At the local hospital," Sheriff O'Neil said.

"Then I'll start there."

Maya had to hope that she would find something. Tomorrow night was the full moon.

CHAPTER FIFTEEN

The medical center was clean, bright, and looked very expensive to Maya. It was the kind of private clinic that kept magazines on property, investments, and yachting in the waiting area, with tasteful artwork on the walls and furniture that reminded Maya more of a high end hotel than a hospital.

The receptionist at the desk certainly looked as polished as any hotel receptionist could have been, with a gloss to her make up and nails that made her look to Maya a little like she'd been laminated.

"Can I help you?"

Maya took out her ID. "I'm here about the death of Cynthia Yoo."

Most people would have been flustered by the sudden appearance of an FBI agent, but it seemed that the receptionist barely even reacted. Of course, now that Maya was closer to her, she could see that at least part of that was because of extensive Botox to eliminate any lines on her face. A glance along the reception counter showed a few leaflets advertising plastic surgery. Maya was willing to bet that was where a lot of the medical center's income came from.

"Do you have an appointment, Agent?" the receptionist asked. "Our staff are very busy."

"No," Maya said. "I was hoping that people here might be able to make time, though. I'd like to talk to the people who worked with Cynthia."

"I'm not sure if that-"

"That will be quite all right, Zara," a woman's voice said.

Maya turned to see a woman of perhaps fifty, dressed in a severe dark suit and white coat, with a stethoscope draped around her neck.

"Yes, Dr. Swanson," the receptionist said.

The newcomer came forward. "Perhaps I can help you, Agent..."

"Gray," Maya supplied, and showed her ID again for good measure. "I'm sorry, you are?"

"Dr. Elaine Swanson, one of the assistant directors of this facility. I also happen to be in charge of our ENT department, where poor Cynthia worked."

That struck Maya as a considerable coincidence, except that she didn't believe in coincidences like that.

"Did Sheriff O'Neil let you know I was coming?" Maya asked. She watched the doctor closely for any reaction to that, but as it turned out, she didn't need to.

"He did," Dr. Swanson said. "I believe he meant it as a way of easing your way here, by asking for our cooperation ahead of time."

Maya wasn't sure whether to be happy about that or annoyed. On the one hand, it was good to run into some local law enforcement that wasn't actively trying to block everything she did. On the other, it meant that the medical center staff had more time to prepare what they would say. Maya wasn't going to be able to startle them into saying anything they shouldn't.

For now, she followed the assistant director up a flight of stairs to a ward that still barely looked like a hospital. There were a couple of spaces that looked like laboratories behind glass screens, but even those looked pristine, as if they were as much about advertising the capabilities of the place as about doing actual medicine.

Dr. Swanson led the way to a room where two doctors and a nurse in scrubs sat, obviously waiting for them. The room seemed to be some kind of staff break room, and it was probably the only part of the hospital that Maya had seen so far that didn't look completely perfect. The chairs were folding ones, rather than expensive hotel furniture. A fridge had post it notes stuck all over it in some kind of silent workplace back and forth, while a board to one side was covered in writing from at least two different hands that Maya could see.

Of the doctors, one was a man in his forties, with buzzcut hair and dark glasses. He was in shape, with large hands whose fingers were neatly entangled with one another. The other was a woman in her twenties, petite, with dark hair, who kept glancing at the board as if she would rather be working on whatever was up there than waiting for Maya. The nurse was a man of about thirty, dressed in scrubs and currently reading a book while he waited.

"Team, this is Agent Gray, with the FBI," Dr. Swanson said. To Maya, it sounded far too close to someone introducing a substitute teacher to a class. "She wants to ask about Dr. Yoo. Please give her any help you can. Agent Gray, this is Doctor Philip Brown, Doctor Adele van Ives, and Head Nurse Sebastian Wiles."

Maya noted that the assistant director stayed in the room. Apparently, while they were going to be free to speak, they were still going to be watched over by their boss.

"What do you want to know?" the older of the two doctors asked.

Maya took a folding chair for herself. "What was Cynthia like? What did she do in her work?"

"Dr. Yoo worked in advanced cochlear implants," the younger doctor, Doctor van Ives, said. "They're used to restore hearing to some individuals with hearing impairments. Dr. Yoo's work means that more people can benefit from them."

"Not everyone can?" Maya said. She wasn't sure if it was relevant, but the more she could get the doctors talking about their former colleague, the better.

"Many people can't benefit from such implants," Doctor Brown said. It sounded to Maya a little like he was delivering a lecture he'd given before. "It depends very much on the type of damage to their hearing. Dr. Yoo pioneered a technique that allowed us to overcome some of the issues with residual damage in the ear rendering implants less effective, so that hearing can be restored to a wider range of people. It has proven very effective."

"Impressive," Maya said. "Also expensive, I assume?"

"The latest treatments often are," Dr. Swanson said. "Costs then come down at a later date."

To Maya, she sounded more regretful about that part than the rest of it. Then again, the clinic's business model probably relied on the costs staying high for as long as possible.

That wasn't the reason she was there, though. She needed to find out if anyone had a reason to kill Cynthia Yoo. One possibility sprang to mind.

"Was Dr. Yoo liked by all of her colleagues?" Maya asked.

The nurse spoke up. "She was great. Always there if anyone needed her. Always willing to go the extra mile."

Maya knew she had to ask the next part, just to be sure. "So there have never been, for example, any accusations of bullying against her?"

"No, of course not!" Doctor van Ives said. "Why would you think that?"

"Hospitals are often very driven environments," Maya suggested. "Sometimes, brilliant people don't have a lot of time for the feelings of others if they don't match up to their standards."

78

The doctors were already shaking their heads, though, almost in unison.

"She wasn't like that," Nurse Wiles said. "I know some surgeons can get a reputation for being difficult, but Dr. Yoo always worked on the basis that a happy team was more productive."

Maya caught his glance over at Dr. Swanson. She guessed that he didn't think she ran things in quite the same way.

"I'm just looking for any motive anyone might have had to want to hurt her," Maya said. "If I can establish that, maybe it will help to narrow down the search."

She hadn't expected someone to just come out and say that she was hated, but it had been a possibility that she'd had to consider. It wasn't inconceivable that there might be a killer out there targeting people he thought had bullied him, given the way Jenette Hiatt had behaved towards the people around her. If Dr. Yoo had been the same way, then that might have been the beginning of a connection between them.

"Do any of you know if she knew a woman by the name of Jenette Hiatt?" Maya asked. It seemed like the kind of thing her colleagues might know. "Did she ever mention her? Did the name ever come up when you were talking?"

Maya could see the answer to that question straight away, in the blank looks she got from the three of them.

"No, nothing like that," Dr van Ives said, then looked slightly puzzled. "Wait, isn't that the name of that woman who was killed by the Moonlight Killer? Do you think Cynthia was murdered by that madman?"

Maya held up a hand to forestall her. "No, I don't. I'm exploring the possibility that there might be some other link. I just want to know if you can remember anything."

Again, the doctor shook her head. "Sorry."

"Can you tell me more about Dr. Yoo's personal life?" Maya asked. "Did she have a partner, a family?"

"I think Dr. Yoo was single," Dr. Brown supplied. "Her family lived down in California somewhere. Honestly, I got the feeling that she was the kind of person who preferred to be alone when she wasn't working."

Which closed off yet more potential connections between her and Jenette. Maya would go back through her messages again, but she was willing to bet that she wouldn't find the doctor's name anywhere in them. They clearly didn't know one another socially.

Which begged the question of what the connection could be, if not that? Maybe that was the wrong way of looking at things, though. Maybe she needed to focus on finding as many avenues that someone might want to hurt the doctor as possible, and only *then* try to find any that connected back to Jenette.

"You say the doctor improved the odds of cochlear implants working," Maya said, "but presumably, some people were still disappointed by the results."

"There are still people they don't work for," Doctor van Ives said. "And of course, there are people whose insurance won't cover them. Because the new procedure isn't well established yet, insurance companies can be reluctant to pay for them."

That sounded like an intriguing possibility. It seemed entirely possible that someone who had been turned down for implants might want to take it out on the doctor who had to deliver the bad news. If that someone had already killed once, maybe they would see that as the obvious solution to their problem.

Maybe there didn't need to be a connection to Jenette Hiatt beyond that.

"Could I get a list of Dr. Yoo's patients?" Maya asked. "Maybe there will be someone on there who-"

"I'm afraid that won't be possible," Dr. Swanson said. "Patient confidentiality requires that we cannot give out that kind of information without a warrant."

"This is a murder inquiry," Maya tried, even though she knew it wouldn't make a difference.

"Even so. If you do get a warrant, we will be happy to help, but otherwise, our hands are tied."

Maya knew that the doctor was only following the rules of her profession, but even so, it was frustrating. In theory, it might be possible to get a warrant, but generally the Patriot Act only allowed the FBI to get medical records like that in cases of suspected terrorism. A mass trawl through medical records on the off chance that there was a killer lurking somewhere in them wasn't going to cut it. She'd put in a request anyway but wouldn't hold her breath.

"Thank you for your time," Maya said, moving to leave. She didn't have any more time to waste here if they weren't in a position to give her any usable information. The full moon was tomorrow, which meant that she needed to find answers quickly if she was going to keep her sister safe.

She needed to find another way to get to the information she needed and find it now.

CHAPTER SIXTEEN

Maya held back her frustration as she left the hospital. She didn't have much time now, and she needed to find another way of figuring out the connection between Jenette and Cynthia.

As she left the hospital, Maya got out her phone and started to compose a request to send over to the FBI headquarters for the warrant. She sent it, but even as she did so, she had the near certainty that she wasn't going to get the information she wanted that way.

So how? Maya went back to her rental car, sat in it, and tried to think. It was easier to do it here than to go back to the precinct in Corvallis. Besides, Maya still wasn't entirely convinced that she was done with Albany.

She needed to work with the information she did have. There had to be a point of connection between Cynthia Yoo and Jenette Hiatt somewhere. She wasn't about to believe that these were just random attacks.

Maya couldn't, because if she did, then there was no way to find the killer. That connection was the way to get to them, so she had to believe that it existed.

Another thought made her believe in it: the fact that the Moonlight Killer had sent her here. Maya knew he was cruel, callous, and deadly, but everything she had seen of him so far suggested that he believed in following rules. He was playing games with her but was playing that game fairly so far. He wouldn't have sent her here if there was no possible way to solve the crime, surely?

Or maybe he had, and now he was going to watch while she failed, while she got her sister killed. That thought brought a moment of panicked horror with it, and Maya had to fight to push it down. She had to believe that she could do something here, or the terror of it all would overwhelm her.

The first step was to try to think of possible connections between Jenette and Cynthia. Maya got out her tablet and started to go through Jenette's messaging account again, looking for any mention of the other woman. If they'd known one another, then that would make this simple.

Maya tried a search for Cynthia's name, but when that came back with nothing, she knew she had to keep going and check for anyone who might be her under a different name. Jenette seemed quite fond of nicknames on her account, all of them cruel. It meant time spent going through each message, looking for anything that sounded medical, anything that might refer to Albany or a hospital.

There was nothing, no one who could have been Cynthia laboring under one of Jenette's ideas of a joke.

Maya went to check Cynthia's social media next. Thankfully, a lot of that still seemed to be up, letting her look through for any sign of Jenette somewhere in the background of any of the pictures she posted, or any mention of her in connection with any of the posts. Again, there was nothing for Maya to find. In frustration, she resorted to just putting both names into a search engine and seeing what came up. Even there, there was almost nothing. No one had even mentioned both murders in the same news article.

There had to be something, but what? These were two women who lived in different cities, who had very different lives and very different jobs. The only connection between them seemed to be that they had both been murdered in exactly the same fashion.

Maya froze as a realization came to her: their jobs weren't entirely unconnected. Jenette had worked in radio, which meant spending time around loud music, wearing headphones. Maybe *that* was the connection.

Before she ran off to check, Maya decided to make sure that her research was good. She started to search for anything she could find relating to hearing loss in the music and radio industry.

This time, there was no shortage of results. Maya quickly read through a scholarly article on the prevalence of tinnitus in the music industry, then skipped over to a piece entitled "Members of classic bands who played it loud (and now don't hear so well)." Maya kept going, but the central point of it all was already clear: people who worked in Jenette's industry had a better than average chance of ending up with some kind of hearing loss.

In other words, as exactly the kind of person who might be one of Cynthia Yoo's patients.

Had *Jenette* been that patient? Maya considered the possibility, but it didn't seem likely. Nowhere in everything Maya had seen about her had it been suggested that she had suffered from any kind of hearing impairment. There had been no mention of signs of any implant in the autopsy files, either. Besides, Maya couldn't even begin to imagine how that would translate into someone wanting to kill them both.

No, it had to be someone else. Someone connected to the radio station, with all the obvious reasons to dislike Jenette, who had also come to hate Dr. Yoo after becoming her patient. Now that she had the glimmer of a connection, Maya could feel her excitement building. She knew where to start with this at last, and she wasn't going to let it go until she had answers. Maybe the people at the hospital couldn't give her everything she needed, but Jenette's colleagues at the radio station didn't have any such limitations.

Starting up the car, Maya headed back towards Corvallis.

*

Radio CorFM turned out to be housed in a tall, glass fronted building near the middle of the town, looking more like an office block than anything else. Then again, Maya had no idea what a radio station's headquarters was meant to look like. It was just that she'd been imagining somewhere a bit more... rock and roll.

There was a security guard on the door, built like a linebacker, with a security vest stretched across his broad frame. He stepped into Maya's path as she approached.

"Maya Gray, FBI. I need to talk to someone about Jenette Hiatt."

Maya showed her ID and saw the security guard look her up and down like he couldn't quite believe that she was who she said she was.

"You can go in," he said.

"Do you have a lot of trouble here?" Maya asked. Given the speed with which the security guard had moved to intercept her, she wanted to know if there was some particular problem around the station that she needed to know about.

"Some," the security guard said. "Some of the radio hosts... well, they call it giving an honest, unfiltered opinion."

"What do you call it?" Maya asked.

84

She saw the security guard shrug. "Shock jock shit. From both ends of the spectrum. We get people here sometimes who aren't happy with something one of them said."

"And that's where you come in?" Maya asked.

He nodded at that. "Sometimes it's not that. Sometimes it's fans. Stalkers, all that kind of thing."

"Did Jenette have any stalkers?" Maya asked.

The guard shrugged again. "Worked behind the scenes. No reason why she would."

Maya guessed he had a point. If she'd been one of the hosts, then it might have been easy to think of her having a target on her back. As it was, probably no one outside of her colleagues had heard of her. In one way, it made things simpler, because it brought them back to the theory that had brought Maya here in the first place.

She headed inside and strode over to a reception desk, showing her ID to the young man working there. He was casually dressed, and so young that Maya guessed he had to be an intern rather than one of their regular staff.

"I need to talk to the station manager," Maya said, firmly.

The receptionist seemed caught off guard by the badge, because he didn't even ask what she was doing there.

"I'll show you up," he said.

He led the way to an elevator, and together, they headed up to the top floor which was given over to a single open plan office that was much more what Maya had expected from the recording industry. There were couches set out around the room so that they would have views over the city, pictures of bands on the walls, and even what seemed to be a few awards stacked up on shelves.

The man who sat at the heart of it all was maybe thirty, wearing a sharp suit that made him look more like a lawyer than anything, with slicked back dark hair and a tan that looked as though it had come out of a bottle.

"Jack, who is this? I don't have any appointments."

"Agent Gray, with the FBI, Mr. Chance," the receptionist said. Maya saw the way he flinched as he said it, obviously nervous thanks to the sharpness in his boss's voice.

"I have some questions about Jenette Hiatt," Maya said, stepping further into the room to make it clear that she wasn't planning to just turn around and leave. She needed help here if she was going to find answers in time.

"Can this wait?" the executive said. "I have a meeting."

"I thought you didn't have any appointments," Maya said, calmly. She caught look of surprise on the executive's face at being caught out. "Please, this won't take long."

"All right, all right. I'm Edward Chance. A pleasure to meet you, Ms. Gray."

He waved her to one of the couches, sitting on the opposite end of it while the receptionist left.

"What do you want to know, Ms. Gray?" Chance asked.

Maya ignored the way he left out her job title, for now. "Jenette Hiatt. I take it you knew her?"

"Of her, certainly," the executive said. "I make it a point to know the names of everyone who works here. I try to know all about them. I want people to feel as if they're part of a family, here at CorFM."

Families, Maya reflected, came in all kinds. From the reaction of the receptionist before, she guessed that this was the kind with a particularly authoritarian father.

"So you would have known if there was anything going on around her at the time of her death?" Maya asked. "Had one of the shows she worked on upset anyone?"

"Well, I don't like to dictate the content of my station's shows," Chance said. "Lively debate punctuated by good music, that's what we're looking for."

Maya was starting to get the feeling that he didn't know nearly as much about his station as he let on.

"I'm sure," Maya said. "When you say you know all about your employees, did you know at the time that Jenette spent her time bullying her colleagues?"

"If any accusations were made, naturally, our human resources department would have taken them seriously," Chance said. "But you have to understand that this is a creative environment, where frank exchanges of views are common."

Maya suspected that meant that he did the legal minimum when it came to protecting his staff, and no more.

"Well, did Jenette have any frank exchanges with anyone in particular?"

She saw the station boss shrug. "I wouldn't know."

86

"But I thought you knew all your staff?" Maya said. She waved that away as if it were nothing, then kept going with the part of all this that she really wanted an answer to. "I'm told that in radio, it's pretty common for people to suffer hearing loss."

"Not that common, whatever the unions say."

Of course he was going to try to avoid what he saw as an accusation. Probably, he didn't want to end up being liable.

"And of course, you do everything possible to minimize the risk," Maya said. "But I imagine there are people who do suffer from it even so."

"Well…" Chance began. "It can happen. A hazard of working in our industry, unfortunately."

"Tell me, can you think of anyone in particular here who has experienced hearing loss? Someone who might have worked with Jenette? Someone who might have sought help for it?"

There was silence for several seconds as Chance thought. Possibly he was thinking about how much he should admit.

"Well, there was Bob Wright. He was an engineer for us. He started to suffer some hearing impairment. Nothing connected to the work, you understand."

Maya understood very well. "Go on."

"Well, in the end, it got so bad that we had to let him go. He kept messing up the mixes. Now I think about it, I believe Jenette may have been the one to bring that to my attention."

Someone Jenette had pushed out to try to further her own career, perhaps? At the very least, this seemed like someone she needed to talk to.

"Do you have an address for him?" Maya asked.

She needed to question Bob Wright, and soon, if she was going to get through this before the deadline.

CHAPTER SEVENTEEN

Maya sat outside the address she had for Bob Wright, observing the small suburban house from across the street. It was in a leafy neighborhood, but the houses around it were relatively small and cheaply built.

It looked as though there was someone home even though there was no car in the driveway, because Maya had caught a flicker of movement through one of the windows. The only question now was how she wanted to play this.

Maya decided that the first thing to do was confirm the connection between Bob Wright and Cynthia Yoo. She ignored another couple of texts from Marco as she got out her phone to call the medical center.

"Hello, could you put me through to Dr. Swanson? This is Agent Gray. We spoke earlier."

She waited for a minute or two.

"This is Dr. Swanson. Agent, if you've called to ask for access to our records, I'm afraid my answer has to remain the same. We cannot do so without a warrant."

"I don't want your records," Maya said. "I just want you to confirm whether one person was a patient of Cynthia's or not. You don't have to tell me anything more than that."

"That would still be a major ethical violation," Dr. Swanson pointed out. "I could be struck off."

"Please," Maya said. "I'm trying to find a killer here, and the only way I can do that is if I find someone who was connected to both of that killer's victims."

"I understand that," Dr. Swanson said. "But that's your job. Mine includes a requirement to keep my patients' details confidential."

"I don't want any medical history, I'm not trying to trawl through your patients; I just need to know whether one man attended your clinic."

Maya knew that she was pushing hard even asking for that much.

"That is still something that I am not meant to disclose," Dr. Swanson said, but Maya could hear the note of uncertainty in her voice.

"This is someone who may have killed one of your colleagues, one of your friends," Maya said, trying to appeal to that personal connection. "The man who murdered Cynthia Yoo is still out there, and you might have the information I need to bring him in."

Even then, Maya thought that Dr. Swanson wouldn't help her. She suspected that the assistant director of the medical center might stick to her rules even though Maya needed her help, even though her sister was in danger.

"Very well," Dr. Swanson said. "I am not comfortable with this, but I believe I can help. What is the name?"

"Bob Wright," Maya said. She kept watching the house. Again, she was sure that she could see movement there. That was good; she didn't want the former sound engineer leaving while she was still trying to establish the truth.

There was a brief pause, presumably as Dr. Swanson looked up the answer.

"Yes, it appears that a man of that name was a patient here. As I said, though, I really cannot tell you more than that."

"That's fine," Maya said. The details almost didn't matter. The point was that there was a man just a short way from her who had a connection to both Cynthia and Jenette.

Her next step was to look over Jenette's messages again. It wasn't hard to find a string of them between her and the man Maya was about to speak to.

WTF was that mix today? I could do better with my fingers in my ears. You think no one around the station knows that you've lost it? Come Monday, I'm talking to Chance.

It wasn't quite a threat to cost Bob Wright his job, but it was pretty close. More than enough of a reason for some people to kill. As for Cynthia… well, if she couldn't help him, that would make him angry too, wouldn't it? Especially if he couldn't afford her fancy new implant.

There was only one way to find out for sure. Maya strode across to the house she'd been watching, raised her hand to hammer on the door, and then thought better of it. Instead, she knocked softly, loud enough that most people would have heard, but not someone who'd suffered a failed implant, or who was angry enough to kill because he'd been turned down outright.

As a result, Maya was pretty surprised when someone answered the door.

The man in front of her was in his late fifties, with shaggy Gray hair and a beard that probably hadn't been trimmed in a year. He was shorter than Maya, with a slight paunch, and he was wearing a t-shirt for a band Maya hadn't heard of over jeans and sneakers. Maya found herself staring at his ears, and in particular at the very faint white scars running alongside them. They were hard to spot, but they were there.

"Hello," he said. "Can I help you?"

Maya showed her ID. "Bob Wright? I'm Agent Gray, with the FBI. I was hoping to talk to you about Cynthia Yoo."

As when she'd knocked on the door, she didn't raise her voice, and again, he obviously heard her perfectly.

"Dr. Yoo? Oh, that was so sad, what happened to her. Please come in."

He showed Maya through to a living room that currently appeared to be at least half workshop, with a table covered by a white cloth in the center, and what appeared to be a deconstructed guitar sitting in the middle of it.

"Please forgive the mess, but I'm just in the middle of making a custom instrument for a young man in… Idaho, I believe it was."

"I'm sorry, you're a guitar builder?" Maya said. "I thought you were a sound engineer?"

"I was," Bob said. Maya caught a brief flicker of regret on his face. "Then my hearing started to go."

"And what happened then?" Maya asked.

"I was let go from my job. It turned out to be the best thing that ever happened to me."

Was that just him realizing what all of this had to be about? Was it just him making sure that Maya didn't have a reason to think that he had a motive? He certainly *looked* happy enough, but maybe he was only happy now. Maybe he'd still been angry enough to kill at the time.

"How was it the best thing to happen to you?" Maya said.

"It gave me time to reassess my priorities," Bob said. "To slow down a little and think about what I wanted to do. Rushing around in radio, getting up at all hours of the morning to mix sound? That's a game for a younger guy than me. I'd always liked guitars, and even if I couldn't hear them as well anymore, I could still work on them. Turns out I was pretty good at it."

"It must still have been difficult, being kicked out of your job like that," Maya said. However much he'd come to terms with it all, that didn't mean he hadn't been angry at the time.

"Well, my kids kicked up a big fuss about it," Bob said. "And that actually worked out pretty well for me. One of them is a lawyer, and she got their legal department to pay out a good chunk of severance. Combine that with money I'd been saving up for a while, and I was finally able to afford to fix my hearing."

"With one of Dr. Yoo's cochlear implants?" Maya said.

She saw Bob nod enthusiastically. "Exactly. When I first started losing my hearing, I was so depressed. It felt as though I was losing the thing that made me who I was. Thanks to her, I can hear pretty much as well as I ever have. I know they say there are some sound distortions with implants, but I swear, these ones make me feel as though I'm hearing the world properly for the first time."

Maya could see the gratitude there, and ordinarily, that would have been wonderful to see. In this case, though, it meant that Maya felt her heart starting to sink. Her one link between Jenette and Cynthia turned out not to have any reason to kill the doctor.

There was still Jenette, of course.

"I believe you worked with Jenette Hiatt," Maya said.

"Worked with her? I'm pretty sure she's the reason I got fired," Bob said. "Horrible person, when she thought she could get away with it. I'm sorry, I shouldn't speak ill of the dead like that, but she was just a bully. Sweetness itself whenever the boss or an important presenter was in the room, but she treated everyone else like they were in her way. I've seen interns crying after they spent the day with her."

"It sounds as though you had plenty of reasons to dislike her."

She saw Bob shrug. "Me and half the station. You don't think I had anything to do with her death, do you? Because I would never do something like that."

Did Maya think he could have had anything to do with it at this point? Honestly, no, for the simple reason that she still thought the two cases were linked. The similarities in method and the proximity of the two killings meant that it made no sense to arbitrarily decide that Jenette might have been killed by the former sound engineer, and Cynthia had been murdered by someone else.

"No, I don't," Maya admitted. "Tell me, was there anyone Jenette argued with more than most? Anyone who might also have known the doctor?"

"I'm sorry," Bob said. "I can't think of anyone. I thought all of that was supposed to be the Moonlight Killer anyway. It was all over the news."

It seemed that everywhere Maya went in Corvallis, there were people telling her that the murders were down to the Moonlight Killer. The problem was that she was having real trouble proving anything else.

Maya still didn't buy it. She knew the Moonlight Killer hadn't done this. The audio world was the connection between the victims; it had to be.

*

Thanks to the journeys back and forth between Corvallis and Albany, it was getting late. Maya returned to her hotel room, working on the files, trying to find another way through all of this. The trouble was that she simply didn't have enough information.

Maya felt certain that some point of connection between Jenette and Cynthia would be the answer to all of this, but she hadn't been able to find one yet beyond Bob Wright. It made sense that someone who had gone to the clinic because of hearing damage sustained through working at the radio station might be the answer, but Bob simply didn't have a good motive.

Just to be sure, Maya put in requests to have the cold cases unit take a closer look at his finances, just in case he'd been lying about the whole process being easy for him. Even so, Maya's instinct was that they would come up with nothing.

Nothing wasn't good enough, not if she wanted to save her sister's life. Her sister and the nine other women still with her were relying on Maya to solve this, to get them away from a man so dangerous that just thinking about him made Maya shiver with fear.

Maya picked up her phone, looking for more texts from Marco in an effort to distract herself from thoughts of the Moonlight Killer. There was nothing new there, though, and Maya wasn't sure what she should even text back at this point. She couldn't help the feeling that she'd messed things up there, too, just like she was doing with this case. She guessed that she could call Marco, but after everything at the restaurant, she didn't want to call him up just to sit talking about how hard the case was while he tried to be sympathetic. He deserved better than that.

She deserved a break in the case. There had to be something, but Maya couldn't see it yet. She knew better than to hope for another clue from the Moonlight Killer too. She got the feeling that he was starting to lose patience with her. Maya would either solve this by the deadline, or a woman would die.

The thought that she might *not* solve it started to creep into Maya then. From the start of this, she'd been determined to find answers, and she'd assumed that the answers would be there to find, or why would the Moonlight Killer send her? Now... now the case had the feel of one of those cold cases that took weeks of careful grinding it down, talking to every contact both of the victims had, looking for that one glimmer of hope.

Maya didn't have weeks, though, and as she started to settle in to sleep, her hope was running pretty thin too.

CHAPTER EIGHTEEN

The hardest thing for Carmel had been to wait, and to plot her way out. The man in the mask let them wander the space he held them in during the daytime, and Carmel was determined to make the most of every moment of it.

Her fear had built throughout the day. What if he noticed that his multi-tool was missing during the day? What if he went searching for it and realized that Carmel had it? He would hurt her at the very least, maybe even kill her.

The hardest thing was not just to drop the multi-tool somewhere and pretend that she'd never seen it. That would be the easy thing, the *safe* thing. The thing that wouldn't risk attracting the masked man's wrath.

Except that nothing here was safe. Carmel could wander this place, go quietly back to her cell every night, and he might still decide to kill her. He might drag her out in front of the others and do to her all the things that he'd done to the quiet one, for reasons that she had no control over.

No, it was better to have her fate in her own hands. It was better to get out of here.

So she walked the confines of their underground prison, trying to assess the best way to get out of there. The other women wandered the place listlessly, some talking to one another, others trying to exercise, a couple just sitting there staring. The one he'd beaten sat with her head against the wall. She caught Carmel's eyes, and there was something piercing about that look, like she *knew* what Carmel was planning.

She gave the faintest shake of her head, but Carmel wasn't going to take advice off some woman who wouldn't even talk to the others. If she thought that just sitting there would get her out of this, then she wasn't paying attention.

Carmel walked the corridors of the space, checking it for anything that would complicate her way out. She saw the soundproofing on the walls, took in the vents there to provide oxygen. There was a stale quality to the air and a sense of pressure that made her suspect that they were underground somewhere. Beyond that, there were no clues as to where they were.

The jumpsuits suggested that their things were stored somewhere. Or maybe they'd just been destroyed. Either way, there would be no time to waste trying to find them. Better just to get out of there and deal with things after that.

She noted where the cameras were. It had been an important skill in her former job. The big door at the end was covered by one, but that was a matter of timing. Cameras only counted when there was someone on the other end of them, watching.

Carmel waited. Eventually *he* came. Carmel froze as he walked in, looking for any sign that he knew what she'd done. When his eyes swept over her, she had to fight to keep any sign of it off her face, force herself not to react.

"Time to go back to your hutches, bunnies!" he ordered.

Carmel went, waiting while he shut her in, fastening the padlock on it. His eyes lingered on her, that cold gaze making her sure that he had seen everything she was planning. Then they passed over her as he went on with his preparations for the night. Eventually, finally, he left, heading out through that big door at the head of their prison. The lights sank to a dim half glow as he did so.

Carmel forced herself to wait after that, counting in her head, trying to judge the time that passed. She left it one hour, then another, giving him time to grow tired. She waited until all the others were sleeping, and then waited some more just to be sure that he wouldn't be sitting in front of his cameras, watching.

Finally, she decided that it was now or never. As terrified as she was, as much as every fiber of her being screamed at her not to do this, Carmel had to act.

Taking the multi-tool, Carmel started to work on the lock, cycling through the attachments until she found ones that would fit inside it. She broke one off to use to hold the tumblers open once she got them in place, then worked with the rest of it.

Her hands were shaking, but she'd lost none of her old skills. In just a minute or two the lock hung open. Better, Carmel had done it silently. None of the others there were awake. That was good, because she didn't want to have to tell them no when they begged to come with her. They would slow her down, and right now, she needed to be fast.

The most she could do was send help later.

Carmel padded through the half dark of the place, moving as quietly as she could, but also determined to move quickly. All it would take was the masked man waking up in the night and glancing at his screens. She had to be out of here before then. The tension of it made her heart thud against the walls of her chest.

She made it to the big air lock style door, with its wheel handle and its oversized lock. Carmel crouched by it, all too aware that she was in full view of another of the cameras. That fact only added to the shakes in her hands as she worked, making her improvised picks lose their bite on the door.

"Calm down, Carmel," she whispered to herself, forcing herself to get back to work on it.

For what seemed like forever, the door held, but then Carmel heard the single most beautiful sound of her life: a dull click as the last tumbler fell into place.

She turned the wheel of the door frantically, pulling it open as rapidly as she could. The door was heavy, and it took an effort to move it, but right then, Carmel's fear gave her strength.

The room beyond looked like some kind of supply room. It had bags of food, while a mask and gloves sat on a shelf off to one side. This was where the masked man prepared before he came in to see them.

There were steps leading up to a trapdoor. Carmel took them and pushed the door open, looking around quickly to make sure that *he* wasn't waiting for her above it. She pulled herself up, into what appeared to be a large wooden cabin, of the kind rich people had built for them on TV when they wanted to "get back to nature" or some bullshit. The whole place looked cozy, comfortable, and completely at odds with those cold eyes that had seemed to look into her soul.

Carmel didn't care. She wasn't there to critique the hand tatted throws or the hunting trophies on the walls. She just needed to get out of there. Still moving quickly, Carmel made her way to the front of the place.

Another locked door stood in her way, but by now, Carmel wasn't going to let something like that stop her. She worked on the lock, and felt it give just as she heard a sound behind her.

She looked around and there *he* was, standing in the dark.

Carmel didn't get a good look at his face, thanks to the darkness, but she saw enough to make her cry out in fear. The features were handsome enough, but those eyes, those eyes seemed to cut through the darkness, fixing on her like a predator sighting its prey.

Carmel hauled the door open, and she ran, not looking back.

The house was set in a clearing, and Carmel saw rabbits scattering in the dark, running back to their burrows as Carmel sprinted past them, heading for the trees. Behind her, she heard the sound of running footsteps, but she didn't look around. She didn't dare. One slip, one trip, and this would be done.

Instead, Carmel increased her pace. She'd always been a good runner, out on the track, and then from the police, or from gangs. This was the same, even if it was for far bigger stakes. She could do this. She *had* to do this.

Carmel reached the tree line, still hearing the crunch of footsteps following her.

"Better if you stop, little bunny," his voice called out.

Carmel didn't believe that for an instant. She'd seen his face now. Getting away was the only option. She dodged between the trees, zigzagging now, hoping to break the line of sight between them. It wasn't enough to run fast; running away was about getting where they couldn't find you, couldn't see you.

Carmel half tripped, caught herself, and kept going. She ducked under a series of low branches, then leapt over a thorn bush, hoping that the obstacles would slow her pursuer down.

Her feet hurt with every step, because she didn't have any shoes. The jumpsuit was baggy and hard to run in. Carmel ignored all of it, because right then there was only being fast enough or dying, doing enough, or failing in the most final way there was.

She ignored the branches that scratched at her cheek. She ignored the twigs that dug into her feet. When she fell again, it hurt, but Carmel forced herself to stand again. She wasn't going to give up, wasn't going to stop running, not here, like this.

Carmel wasn't sure how long she kept running for, but slowly, she became aware that the sounds of pursuit behind her had started to fade. Even then, Carmel didn't stop, because she knew there was too much of a chance that it might all be a trick, designed to slow her down.

She *did* risk a glance behind her. She saw nothing, no sign of anyone following, no shadows that might have been *him* coming after her. Had she done it? Had she actually lost him?

Relief vied with wariness inside Carmel, and she kept moving. She had no idea where she was right then; the only thing she could think about was trying to put as much distance as she could between herself and the cabin. Even that worried her a little, because she'd heard the stories of people who couldn't see their way in the woods just walking in circles until they ended up back where they'd started.

She couldn't afford to go back. She had to keep going.

Carmel could feel her breath coming shorter with the effort of running for so long, but ahead, she could see a break in the trees. Carmel approached it and stopped for a moment or two, looking down. There, beneath her feet, sat the tarmac of a road.

Now, Carmel's heart leapt. A road meant a connection to civilization. A road might even mean cars that she could flag down and ask for help. A road meant that she wasn't going to be stuck alone in the woods forever, because whichever direction she chose, eventually there would be a town of some description. She was still afraid, but there was a chance now, at least. There was the hope that if she just kept going, she would be able to get to safety.

After that, she would call the cops. She would bring them back, and they would drag the man in the mask out of his cabin like the scum he was. Better yet, maybe they would shoot him, and Carmel would be able to watch him get what he really deserved.

For now, the only question was which direction to go in. Left or right? There was nothing to choose between them, so Carmel picked right. She set off jogging along the smooth surface of the road, and even though it was hard, she kept going, every pace taking her a step closer to safety.

CHAPTER NINETEEN

The man they called Frank watched his bunny jogging her way down the road, and he felt the familiar cold anger building in him. The same anger that couldn't be assuaged in any other way when it came to the nights of the full moon.

In this case, the anger was mixed with a certain satisfaction. He'd judged which way Carmel was going to go perfectly, so that now, she wasn't running away from him anymore, but running right towards the spot where he stood in silence among the dark of the trees.

A poor hunter chased. A good hunter waited.

Frank was good at waiting, and even better at hunting. He waited as Carmel approached, jogging towards… what? Did she think that safety lay in that direction? People were so predictable sometimes.

Frank let her get level with him, watching the fear on her face, along with the determination. He let her go past, let her take a couple more steps before he moved.

Frank started towards her, moving swiftly through the trees. Before, he had been willing to see just how far his bunny could hop out of her cage, but now, it was time to put an end to this.

He brushed through the trees like a ghost. He'd made more sound before, but that had been intended to scare her. Here, like this, he was silent. Carmel didn't even look around as he closed on her.

There was no question of letting her go, no question of letting her *live*. For one thing, she'd seen his face, even if it had been shrouded in darkness. For another, she had broken the rules, and breaking the rules should always be punished.

That wasn't the real reason, though. The *real* reason was the need rising in him. The dark need that could only be satisfied one way.

He closed on Carmel, and in that last stride she looked around to see him, obviously hearing the scrape of his boot on the road. He could see the terror on her face in that moment, and in that second, she really did seem like a bunny, watching an eagle descend and unable to do anything about it.

Frank threw himself at her, his weight slamming into her, bearing her to the ground. That was one of the first things he'd learned: to strike fast, not to give them any time to even think about fighting back.

He felt the impact as the two of them hit the ground and heard the whoosh of air coming out of Carmel's lungs as Frank's weight fell atop her. He was braced for it in a way that she wasn't, already moving while she scrabbled around, trying to work out what she should do.

Frank could feel the blood pulsing inside him then. In moments like this, he felt alive in a way he didn't most of the rest of the time.

She fought back, or tried to. Sometimes they did. It never made any difference. Most people weren't good at fighting at the best of times, but in the dark, taken by surprise? Frank fended off her attempts to lash out at him with her fists and fetched his stun gun from his belt. He heard Carmel cry out as he used it on her, twitching in pain.

He pulled a short length of rope out of one of his pockets. It was nylon stranded bungee cord, simple and strong. The moment he'd felt it against his fingers the first time, he'd known that it was perfect for what he wanted.

Frank wrenched Carmel over onto her stomach. She screamed, but out here there was no one to hear it. Certainly not anyone who could get here to help. She tried to get her hand up to block the cord as he pulled it over her head, but he'd done this too many times for that to work. He pulled her hands out of the way, whipping the ligature into place in one clean movement.

Frank saw her scrabbling for something and saw the moment when her hand came out with his own multi-tool, blade attachment already extended. She stabbed for him, and if she'd been more accurate, that might have been an end to him, but instead, the blade just scraped along Frank's ribs.

Frank roared in anger and smashed her hand against the ground, knocking the weapon out of Carmel's grip. He tossed it to the side, where it wouldn't be a threat, and as Carmel tried to get to it, he used his weight to pin her in place.

Frank got both of his hands onto the rope and started to pull it tight.

There were so many ways to kill someone: shooting, poisoning, stabbing, blowing them up with explosives, running them down with a vehicle. Frank had looked at them all, considered them all. He'd even learned a few at the hands of professionals. Yet for him, nothing compared to the personal touch of strangulation, the neatness of a rope

100

around a neck, feeling the struggles of a victim relayed through the weapon that was killing them.

Carmel's hands went to the rope, because that was what they all did once it went tight. She clawed at it as if there might be a way to get under it, but Frank had pulled it far too tight for that. He put a knee in the small of her back, giving himself more leverage, not letting up the pressure even for an instant.

Frank got annoyed when he saw depictions of strangulation on TV. They always got it wrong, always showed the neck snapping in some sudden, ludicrous way. That wasn't the point of it, wasn't the satisfaction of it. *That* came from the fading struggles of his victim, from Carmel thrashing spasmodically and those spasms growing weaker.

She went still as she fell into unconsciousness, but Frank kept his grip. Killing someone took longer than the few seconds it took to put them out.

It was also the part that he found the most special. Anyone could experience the moments leading up to unconsciousness, could be strangled into it and then come back. Anyone could take someone that far. They could know what it was like. Only he knew the subtle feeling of the changes as Carmel went from a living person to a dead thing. Only he had felt it time and again, so that he knew the moment of death as perfectly as he knew night from day.

Frank felt the last shuddering gasp of the body, and it was done.

Another time, and there might have been more satisfaction in it as he stood, looking down at her body. This was normally the moment when he left them to be found, walked off and let the rest of the world deal with the aftermath. This was normally one of the few truly peaceful moments Frank knew.

This moment, though, was anything but peaceful. There were feelings intruding on it that normally had no place in this. Not guilt or remorse, of course. Those were weaknesses for lesser people, but… disappointment? Yes, disappointment, dissatisfaction, anger.

This hadn't been the plan. This hadn't been how any of this had been meant to go. None of his bunnies should have been able to escape, and yet this one had. Now, he'd had to kill her, when there had been no failure by dear Maya to warrant it. It left him short a bunny.

There were also more immediate concerns. He was injured, even if it wasn't much, and that would need to be tended to. Then there was the matter of a body too close to his house. The last thing Frank needed was someone spotting her here and then checking to see where she might have come from. No, he had to deal with all of this, and dealing with the aftermath of killings wasn't something he normally did.

Frank started by collecting his multi-tool, on the basis that he didn't want anything with his fingerprints and DNA just lying around. Tucking it in his belt, he went to Carmel's body and lifted her easily, carrying her over one shoulder as he stepped back into the forest. He wasn't bothered by any blood on the ground. It would rain soon enough to wash that away.

He made his way back through the trees, keeping well away from any tracks. There shouldn't be anyone out there at night, but the last thing he needed was to run into some nighttime hunter, who might shoot as soon as he saw Frank with the body. He padded back through the dark, brain already working out the best way to deal with all of this.

He needed to find a way to get some use out of Carmel's death. His bunny wouldn't cheat him of that much.

Frank returned to his cabin, carrying the corpse down through the trapdoor. He put on his mask and gloves. The other bunnies were all in their cells, so he wouldn't need his stun gun for this, but he brought it anyway. He turned the lights up fully. He wanted them to see this.

He strode in, carrying Carmel's body to the space in front of their hutches.

"Wake up!" he bellowed. This was no time for even the illusion of kindness.

He threw Carmel's corpse down in front of them as they roused from sleep, let them stare. A couple of them screamed at the sight. People were so *weak*.

"Be quiet!" he snapped, glaring around at them for a second or two before he got himself under control. He switched to his jovial voice, although even he could hear the undercurrent of cold anger that was still there. "One of you has been a very naughty bunny. She tried to hop all the way out of our little warren. She paid the price for it. I've shown you before, and I'll tell you it openly now: there is no way out of here. You will sit and be good bunnies, and if you're lucky, you'll be let go. But if you break the rules…"

He gestured to Carmel and left her there as he went through to the control center he kept further along in the bunker. It was a large, round room, with banks of monitors on one wall. Currently, one of them was tuned to a security camera outside a hotel room in Oregon.

Frank went to a box by one wall, getting out a first aid kit. The wound at his side was shallow, but he would probably need to stitch it. That was fine, nothing he hadn't done before. His mind was barely even on it as he started to clean out the wound.

Instead, his mind was on Maya. What would she think of tonight's little adventure? How would she react? Would it be better to simply lose the body somewhere in the woods, never to be found?

No, there were too many risks in that, and there were still things that could be achieved with the right kind of display. The question was where. Frank started to pull up maps, trying to think of the perfect place. Somewhere not too far from Maya, this time. He wouldn't want her getting overly distracted.

And he would need to explain things. That was only right.

Carefully, he extracted another box. It held plain rectangles of cards, artists' brushes, and pens. Drawing was another of those skills that people seemed to make so much of, but that Frank had found easy to acquire once he put his mind to it. It was yet another thing that hadn't done anything to reduce the need he felt to kill.

He drew carefully, sketching out the bunny the way he wanted it and letting it dry while he monitored his favorite FBI agent. She would be sleeping now. He wondered if she dreamed of him. Frank didn't remember his dreams, but he suspected that if he had them, Agent Gray would feature in them.

Her, and possibly a strangling rope.

Flipping over the card, Frank started to write.

CHAPTER TWENTY

Maya was running through a maze, taking twists and turns on instinct, trying to find her sister.

Desperation filled her. She knew that Megan was somewhere there ahead, but the harder she tried to find her, the more complex the maze seemed to become, branching until it seemed impossible to guess the correct way to go.

Then there were the puzzles.

Maya found the first of them standing there on a chalkboard, propped up on an easel. Some math problem she vaguely remembered from school. A postcard was stuck to it, only this one didn't depict cute bunny rabbits. This one had an image of Megan, dangling above some impossible drop, moving like it was a camera feed taken live.

Maya knew that she had to solve the puzzle, but somehow, the math seemed to be swimming there on the chalkboard, making it hard to pin down exactly what the problem even was. The parts she could make out, she couldn't remember, no matter how hard she tried, and that seemed wrong, because she was sure it was stuff that she knew.

A sand timer appeared next to the board, just hanging there. Grains fell through it far too quickly, disappearing with every glance Maya took at the board. She tried to disentangle the lines of the problem, but it wouldn't come, it wouldn't…

The sand ran out, and Maya screamed as her sister fell.

But it didn't end there, somehow. Instead, she found herself walking on, sure that Megan was just a little way ahead, in spite of what she'd just seen. She turned another corner, and there was another puzzle set out…

*

Maya woke in a cold sweat to the early morning light. The memories of her dream were far too vivid: seeing Megan die, again and again, because of puzzles that had been impossible to solve.

It didn't take her psychological training to work out where *that* had come from.

The truth was that she was running out of time on this case. Tonight was the night of the full moon. The Moonlight Killer had said that if she didn't solve the case by tonight, *two* women would die. Did that mean two bunnies, or one of his captives and someone else? If so, was he threatening to kill them, or did he mean that whoever had killed Jenette and Cynthia had another victim in mind?

Maya didn't know. More than that, she didn't know *anything* for sure on this case. One more day wasn't enough time, not to solve the whole thing, when she barely had any leads beyond a sense that the deaths of Jenette Hiatt and Cynthia Yoo were connected.

Maya got up, knowing that she had no choice but to get started. That was when she saw an all too familiar shape poking under the door to her room. A postcard sat there, waiting for her, obviously pushed under the door during the night by whoever the Moonlight Killer got to do his dirty work for him.

The sight of it fanned the lingering embers of dread from the dream into life. Maya rushed over to pick it up, staring at the picture, of a single bunny rabbit sitting in what appeared to be a bubbling bath, reading some kind of treasure map. She had no doubt that the whimsy of it meant something to the Moonlight Killer, but Maya couldn't work out what.

It made more sense when she turned over the card.

Bigelow Hot Springs. Come alone this time. No more games.

Maya's first thought was that it had to be some kind of trap, and that Harris had been right all those times he'd said that the kidnapper's endgame was to get to her. Then Maya considered the postcards, the ease with which the Moonlight Killer had already been able to get into her life. This was something else.

Maya had a horrible, sinking feeling as she considered what that might be. Quickly, she looked up the location of Bigelow Hot Springs. It was a couple of hours' drive from her. Going there and back would use up hours of this last, precious day, yet Maya felt as though she didn't have a choice. The Moonlight Killer called, and Maya had to come running, had to run all the twisted paths of his game, because her sister was in danger if she didn't.

Dressing and grabbing her things, she ran for the door.

The hot springs were a small nature reserve off the McKenzie River. All Maya could see as she approached were the surrounding trees, and the river running by, shallow and a bright blue that might have been relaxing if Maya hadn't been sure that she was driving towards something either dangerous or horrifying.

She pulled up in the parking lot that had been put in place to allow access to the hot springs. There were a couple of other cars there, probably tourists. That begged the question of where exactly the Moonlight Killer wanted Maya to go. It wouldn't be somewhere with people around, wouldn't be anywhere with a chance of someone other than her finding it.

She took a closer look at the postcard, thinking about the small treasure map on the front. It was too small to look at properly, so Maya took out her phone and took a photograph of it, as close as possible, then zoomed in on the image until just that section filled her entire screen.

She wasn't entirely surprised to find a level of detail there that she might have found on a real map, with contour lines and trees drawn in, making it obvious that this was a map of a real place.

This place. Maya called up a map of the surrounding area, and quickly saw that the two were identical. The contour lines made it like staring at two identical fingerprints.

The only difference was that the one on the postcard had an X on it in red, with a dotted line leading to it, obviously showing the route that Maya should take. Maya felt a flash of anger at that. He'd plotted out every step of her journey for her, just another way of showing that he was in control of all of this.

Maya looked around, trying to orient herself. There were trees all around, and rock formations sticking up through them along the banks of the river. Those and the river were the easiest things to use to get a sense of which way around everything was.

It took a few seconds, but Maya quickly established that she wasn't going in the direction of the main spring. Instead, the route seemed to lead down a track that seemed almost disused, half covered with foliage, so that Maya had to push her way through.

The perfect place for an ambush.

As soon as that thought came to Maya, she drew her Glock, wanting to be ready. If anyone leapt out at her here, there would be no time to get to it otherwise. That having it in her hand helped to assuage some of the fear that was building up inside her had nothing to do with it. Ok, maybe a little.

Maya scanned the space around her, moving slowly now, feeling the crunch of pebbles underneath her shoes as she eased her way forward. The trees provided glimpses of the river beyond, but Maya was more concerned with trying to spot any sign of someone there waiting for her.

It wasn't enough to just look for movement, her military training had taught her that much. Someone could stay still, use camouflage, and be almost invisible if you weren't looking closely. She had to be systematic, scanning the surrounding trees, ignoring the tension rising in her chest.

It wasn't just the possibility of a killer waiting for her that made Maya look closely. It would be easy to hide a tripwire among the debris of the track's stony ground, or to hide a pressure plate, waiting for Maya to step on it.

Given what the Moonlight Killer had done in the houses he'd lured the FBI to before, it was more than possible. There could be a trap waiting for her with any step she took, so Maya had to plan every step, check that it was safe, and only then put her foot down with the greatest of care.

Step by step, having to force herself to keep breathing normally, having to push down the fear she felt, Maya followed the Moonlight Killer's map.

The trees opened out ahead of Maya, leading up to what seemed to be another hot spring. There were trees around it, hemming it in and shielding it from view, while the river ran along in front of it, bubbling past on a bend sheltered by a couple of large rocks on the far side, so that again, it would be hard to see this spot.

A woman's body lay by the spring, dead or unconscious.

Maya gasped at the sight, even though she'd been half-expecting, half-dreading, this. The woman lay there, turned away from her so that it was impossible to see her face. She was dark haired and slightly built, and Maya felt a moment of pure terror then.

What if this was Megan? What if the Moonlight Killer had tired of his game, and killed her simply because he could?

107

Maya ran forward then, all thoughts of danger forgotten. If that was her sister there, then nothing else mattered, only getting to her, only Megan.

Maya reached the body's side, and it was obvious as soon as Maya got close that the woman lying there had been dead for some time. Maya knew that she shouldn't contaminate the crime scene, shouldn't touch the body at all, but even so, she couldn't stop herself from rolling the corpse onto her back, wanting to see, wanting to know.

It wasn't Megan.

Relief flooded through Maya even as dead eyes stared up at her. Her growing panic subsided for a second, because it wasn't her sister lying there; it was a stranger's face, not one she knew.

That relief was only brief, though, because she was still looking at the features of a dead young woman, someone the Moonlight Killer had murdered, one of his bunnies.

"Why?" Maya called out to the forest around her. She assumed that he would be watching and listening. He wouldn't want to miss a moment like this, would he? She had no doubt that he was there somewhere, or that there was a camera trained on all of this, so that he could enjoy every moment of Maya's torment.

"Why?" Maya repeated. "What did I do wrong?"

He wanted Maya to follow his stupid rules, wanted her to play his game, and threatened to kill if she didn't go along with it. Yet he wasn't playing by those same rules.

He'd killed one of the women he held captive, and Maya couldn't see a reason for it. That was a terrifying thought in itself, because if she couldn't predict what the serial killer was going to do, how could she be sure if he would keep his word on anything now?

Was all of this meant as a threat, a warning? Something else?

The other question at this point was what Maya was supposed to do next. Was she meant to just go back to Corvallis after this? Was she meant to go back to working on the Moonlight Killer's task for her without knowing if it would save anyone?

No, she had to keep going. Even if she couldn't be certain about what the Moonlight Killer would do, solving this was the only hope Maya had of saving her sister.

There was one other thing she knew she had to do now, and it was a hard one. The moment she called this in, Maya knew there was going to be trouble. Harris and the rest would be all over this, and they wouldn't react well to this death that seemed to undermine the rules of the Moonlight Killer's game.

Even so, Maya didn't have a choice. Getting out her phone, she called the office.

"This is Agent Maya Gray. I'm in Bigelow Hot Springs, and I've just found a body."

CHAPTER TWENTY ONE

All Maya could do was sit on a rock and watch while FBI technicians and agents swarmed like ants over the site where she'd found the body of the young woman.

Maya felt a strange kind of grief as she watched them work, taking photographs and making measurements. She was responsible for this, somehow. She was sure of it.

Her, or her bosses.

Had Harris tried another raid? Had Reyes found another possible location for the kidnapper? Had they gone blundering into another trap set by the Moonlight Killer? Would they really have done that without so much as telling her?

Maya knew that they might have. It was increasingly obvious in all of this that her colleagues had very different objectives than she did. They wanted to catch the kidnapper, regardless of what it took. Maya wanted to save the women he had as his prisoners. She wanted to save her sister.

There was a reason she hadn't told them that the Moonlight Killer was behind all of this. That would be enough to drive them to chase him, even if it got every one of his captives killed. They'd reason that the risk was worth it to bring down the most dangerous serial killer still at large.

Maya couldn't let them take that kind of risk with Megan's life, with any of their lives. The way to deal with this was to solve the case.

"How much longer?" Maya asked one of the agents there. She wanted to get back to Corvallis. Every second that she spent here was time that she didn't have to solve the case.

"We still need a full statement from you about what happened, Agent Gray," the agent said.

"Then feel free to take that statement," Maya replied. "I'm running out of time. I have a deadline to solve a case. If I don't finish it by tonight, another woman will die."

The need to get back filled her then, but there was also guilt that came along with it. This might not be because of Harris and the rest.

This might be because the Moonlight Killer knew that she was failing to solve the case. The last time she'd been like this, he'd sent her a clue. Maybe this time, he'd decided to motivate her in a more brutal way.

The thought that this might be because of her brought anger, but also a sick feeling in Maya's stomach.

"I've been asked to wait," the agent said. "Deputy Director Harris wants to do this himself."

As if the words had summoned him, Harris strode into the clearing. For once, his avuncular demeanor was gone. He was dressed in an FBI tactical jacket, looking as though he was getting ready to go on a raid rather than dropping in on a crime scene from across the country.

What must it have taken to get him here so quickly? Flights, certainly. Probably a helicopter on top of that. All so that he could stand in front of Maya, striding up in front of her rock, looking angry and disappointed all at once.

"What the hell is going on here, Gray?" he demanded. He waved a hand at the spot where forensics were starting to move the woman's body to a body bag. "What is all this?"

"I'm not sure, sir," Maya said. "The kidnapper sent me a postcard, and it led me here. I found the body here."

"And you didn't think to call this in *before* you came to a potentially dangerous location?" Harris *really* didn't look happy now. He was red faced with it, obviously building up to some sort of outburst.

"The card he sent specified that I was to come alone. I didn't want to endanger any of his hostages by disobeying him. Again."

Maya couldn't stop herself from including that last word or keeping a note of accusation out of her voice. It was only one word, but it carried with it all her frustrations at the ways Harris and the others had jeopardized things before by going after the kidnapper.

"And how has that worked out for you?" Harris shot back, with another pointed glance towards the body.

"I didn't know what I would find here," Maya said. "But I couldn't take the risk-"

"With your sister in this maniac's hands. Yes, I know." Harris's tone was hard, without a hint that he was giving her any leeway because of it. "I'm starting to think that's a problem, Agent Gray. You're acting like a sister, rather than an agent."

111

"I'm trying to solve crimes. I *am* solving crimes."

That was one part of this that he wouldn't be able to deny. Maya had solved two murders already because of all this. She'd saved two women.

"By any means necessary, from what I hear," Harris said. He waved away the agents nearby. That was a bad sign, when he'd been willing to do the rest in front of them. "I had a call from the federal prison at Pollock, Louisiana. They say that you broke a man's arm and then used it to force him to give you the information that led you to Eddie Chavez."

Maya had known that she would have to defend herself on that count at some point, but she hadn't thought that it would be here, like this, when she was still reeling from finding the body of a woman who shouldn't have died.

Even so, she tried her best.

"Did they also mention the part where he had tried to stab me in the seconds before that? I broke his arm because otherwise he might have killed me."

"The guard with you mentioned that part. He also says that you could have let go then."

"In his opinion," Maya said.

Harris gave her a steady look that said he saw through that easily. "Do you understand how much leeway I've given you on all of this, Gray? Do you understand how much I've had your back? The only reason you aren't facing disciplinary action right now is because there's no camera footage from the prison to show things either way. It's your word against a guard's."

"In a situation where anything up to lethal force might have been justified," Maya replied. "Besides, without the information he gave us, we wouldn't be any closer to catching the guy who did this."

"We *aren't* any closer," Harris snapped. "And now, he's done something like this. Why?"

"I don't know," Maya admitted.

"You don't know? That's not good enough, Gray. If there's no reason for this, then your little arrangement with this psycho means nothing."

Maya stood. "It means that we've gotten back two women so far."

"And a third is dead. Why? Because you're not solving this fast enough, or just because he wanted to kill someone? Our best option now is to stop playing his game and put all our resources into catching him."

Maya couldn't allow that to happen. She *wouldn't* allow that to happen.

"There are still nine more women being held by him, sir."

"Including your sister, which makes you too close to all of this to make decisions about it."

Harris took a step back, like he might just walk off and go start planning a raid. As though nothing she said *meant* anything at this point.

"If we do things your way, nine women will die," Maya said, loud enough that it carried. She didn't care who heard her. In fact, she wanted them to hear, so that Harris couldn't throw away lives without others knowing about it. "We don't have the evidence to find who did this, and he's been one step ahead of us in any case every time. The *only* way we get anyone else back is if I go back to Corvallis and solve the murder of Jenette Hiatt."

Harris turned, and Maya thought then that she'd gone too far. His anger was written in every hardened line of his face, in the sudden squareness of his posture, in everything about him.

But the point was that she was right.

"Very well," Harris said, after several long seconds. "Go back and solve this. But if you don't manage it in time, you're done. I'll transfer you to another department, but you won't go near this case again."

Which meant that now Maya had no choice other than to solve this; and coming here had already eaten hours out of the day. She had to get back to Corvallis.

*

In the office they'd given her in the Corvallis PD, Maya ran through the files in desperation. She had the file on Jenette and the one on Cynthia open side by side, looking for anything that she'd missed, but she couldn't see anything.

Already, half the day was gone. Tonight was the night of the full moon. Tonight was the night when someone was meant to die, but a woman had *already* died today, and Maya couldn't push that fact out of her mind. It intruded on her attempts to focus, filling her with a mixture of grief, anger and frustration.

113

She needed to talk to someone about this, but her boss had already shown that he was in no mood to talk. The local detectives were ok, but they wouldn't understand all of this. That left only one person.

Getting out her phone, Maya called Marco.

It was half a dozen rings before he picked up, and even then, his voice sounded anything but his usual friendly, cheerful self.

"Hi, Maya. Is something wrong?"

Just the question was almost enough to push Maya over the edge and into tears. She held them back, but barely. She wasn't going to spend every conversation around Marco breaking down in front of him.

"It's... there's a lot happening here. I have a murder to solve, I don't have any leads, and I only have a few hours to do it. I need to talk it through with someone."

"And you immediately thought of me." Marco didn't sound happy about it. "You haven't replied to any of my messages for days, Maya."

"I... I was busy." Didn't he understand the kind of pressure she was under?

"And I'm busy now. I've had a double homicide come in, possibly gang related. You know as well as I do that the first forty-eight hours are the most crucial in any investigation."

He wasn't going to help her? "If I don't solve this, then a woman could die."

"And if *I* don't solve my case, then there could be a gang war in my city," Marco replied. "I'm sorry, Maya. I want to help where I can, but you can't just treat me as someone you ignore, and then expect me to drop everything the moment it's convenient for you."

"I..."

"Look, I'm sorry, I have to go. I've got witnesses coming in, and I need to talk to them before anyone else. Whatever this is, I'm sure you can solve it, Maya. I've seen you do it before."

He hung up. He actually hung up on her. Maya sat there staring at her phone for more than a minute, willing Marco to call her back. He didn't, though. She was just left sitting there with her thoughts, trying to make some sense of all of this.

It didn't make sense, though. Someone had killed Jenette Hiatt. Probably the same someone had killed Cynthia Yoo, but Maya didn't know what the connection was. She didn't know where to look, and she didn't have enough time to simply trawl through every facet of their lives until she found something.

Maya had never felt as alone as she did in that moment.

The worst part was that it didn't make a difference. This case didn't care how she felt, or how much pressure was on her. The Moonlight Killer wasn't about to make exceptions just because it was all getting too much for Maya, and she suspected that neither was Harris.

Maya had to find an answer by tonight, or another woman was going to die.

CHAPTER TWENTY TWO

From his van, he listened and he watched. The world around him spread out in a soundscape provided by his speakers. He heard footsteps, phone calls, the sounds of his main target as she worked. He could picture Cindy there with her colleagues, hear her usual routes around her workplace, as easily as if he were standing next to her.

It wasn't her he was watching, though. Not right now. Instead, he sat outside the local police precinct, observing. It was important to spend as much time on them as on his target. There couldn't be any surprises when the moment came. He watched the comings and goings from the building making notes, observing timings.

He saw the moment when the FBI agent showed up, later than he would have thought she might. Listening in to the supposedly private channels of the police provided an answer to that one though.

"...something about a body. FBI stuff."

"Here? Because that makes it *our* stuff."

"Out of town somewhere. I had a call said something about some hot spring a couple of hours east."

East? What was the agent doing investigating something so far out of the city? Did she think it was connected to him? Was she that far off track?

"Not our problem then."

She *was* a busy agent, wasn't she? He watched as she walked towards the building, and today it seemed that her head was down, not looking around her. Even from this distance, she looked upset.

On another day, he might have felt a little sorry for her, trudging in to work like that. He knew what it was like to have a bad day. The emotions of an FBI agent weren't his problem, though, only what she knew, and didn't know.

It was harder listening in inside a police precinct than in someone's home, but not *much* harder. For all that it was a place filled with Corvallis's finest; it wasn't as though they actively expected surveillance, and it didn't take much beyond trial and error to get a shotgun microphone pointed at the right window. It didn't take much more than that to tap into a phone feed.

That was what people got wrong about surveillance. They assumed that it took some particular cleverness or cunning, when what it mostly took was patience. There was no one more patient than he was. Hadn't he waited months between each killing, because a spree wouldn't look like the work of the Moonlight Killer? Hadn't he watched each of his targets carefully, precisely, before he took them? Thanks to the gear he'd bought for his van, most of it legally, some of it on the dark web, he was a spider sitting in the middle of its web, listening to the vibrations along every strand.

Currently, he was listening to the FBI agent make a phone call.

"It's... there's a lot happening here. I have a murder to solve, I don't have any leads, and I only have a few hours to do it. I need to talk it through with someone."

The shotgun mic didn't give him the other side of the conversation, but right then, he didn't need it. All he needed were those five little words: "I don't have any leads."

Those words meant that he was safe. Briefly, when the agent had come to town, he'd been worried, because he'd taken the time to look up Agent Maya Gray. He'd found out a lot about her. He'd read about her military background, about her psychological training, about her career working for the cold cases unit. He'd read about the cases she'd solved, and the recent ones had been particularly worrying. Two arrests in a matter of weeks where she had shown that cases previously attributed to the Moonlight Killer hadn't been him at all?

Given what he was doing here, that had been worrying. It had suggested that she knew something, and that it might lead to her finding out the truth. It said that she was there specifically for him. He'd been trying to decide if he should do something about her before he finished this.

Now, with just a few little words, it seemed that he didn't need to.

She didn't have any leads, and by now, there was no time for her to solve anything. Even in the unlikely event that she found something out now, it would be too late to stop him. He could finish this, and then disappear, if he had to. Judging by the way Agent Gray was talking, it probably wouldn't even be necessary.

That brought with it a sense of deep satisfaction. There was something fulfilling, something complete, about knowing that he was in a position to finish this. He had put so much work into this. He had spent so much time watching, so much time listening. He had prepared for it all so perfectly and put so much of his life into it.

Returning his attention to his target, he drove off. It was her he needed to focus on now, not on an FBI agent who didn't have any thread to pull on that might lead to him. He would keep an eye on her, of course, and on the police, but it seemed that he didn't have anything to worry about.

Tonight, he would strike again, and Agent Gray wouldn't be able to do anything to stop him.

CHAPTER TWENTY THREE

The easiest thing in the world would have been for Maya to sit there feeling sorry for herself. She had so little time left now, and it seemed impossible that she might find an answer in time. Even Marco didn't seem to want to help her, although after the way Maya had ignored him before, she kind of got it.

She was alone, but she still had to find a way to do this. She needed to get into the killer's mind. She needed to work out the kind of man he was. *That,* at least, was something she was good at.

Maya got up and walked out of the office. It was doing her no good just sitting there like that. As she walked out, she saw Bennet and Collingwood heading over, neither of them looking hopeful by this point that Maya was going to give them anything worthwhile to do.

"Where are you going?" Bennet asked.

"Nowhere," Maya said, continuing to walk. "I just think better when I'm moving."

Or at least, it helped to drive away some of the thoughts about how all of this had been going wrong.

"I think Chief Strauss prefers us to work in our assigned spaces," Collingwood said.

Maya gave him a look and kept walking. The police chief had been generous here, but Maya needed to do things her way. She wasn't entirely surprised when the two detectives fell into step with her. At least it gave her someone she could bounce ideas off of.

"I want to get into the head of the killer," Maya said.

"The Moonlight Killer is-" Collingwood began. Apparently, he was still determined to cling to that idea.

"*Not* the Moonlight Killer," Maya said. "Someone pretending to be him. The sites where the bodies were left were display sites, and they did a good job of mimicking the Moonlight Killer, but the very fact that they moved the victims doesn't fit the pattern."

"Ok," Bennet said, keeping pace as they rounded a corner. "But by that logic, we can't learn anything about the killer from those sites. Anything there was just there to try to copy the Moonlight Killer."

119

That was true, although it told Maya plenty in itself.

"It tells us that whoever did this prepares well. He plans. He wants to get away with it, and he feels he needs a deflection to do it. *He* thinks there's too much of a chance of identifying him if we look closely."

"At a golf course?" Collingwood said. They squeezed past a detective coming out of an office, who gave them a disapproving look as they moved on. It seemed that Chief Strauss really did like people to stay in the spaces he gave them.

"Not at the dump sites, at the actual murder scenes. Those are where he chose to kill, so they have to say something about his personality."

"But you *looked* at the alley," Bennet pointed out. "It wasn't anything, just Jenette Hiatt's usual way back from the bar she went to."

Something snagged in Maya's brain, something that it took her a moment to latch onto properly. It made her stop so suddenly that the other two almost ran into the back of her.

"Say that again?" Maya said.

"Say what?" Bennet looked confused. "You know that Jenette Hiatt was killed outside a bar already."

"Not just a bar," Maya said. "Her usual bar. And the alley behind it was her usual way back home. It was a shortcut that she always took."

"And?" Bennet said.

"So Cynthia Yoo was dragged into an alley while on her way to a restaurant, in a perfectly chosen site with no cameras, no witnesses. How did he know that she would go past that spot? He couldn't have seen from the street that it would be good for him, and she wouldn't have gone that way on any other day. How did he know that Jenette always took one particular shortcut home from a bar?"

"You're saying he watched them?" Collingwood said.

"Surveillance," Maya said. "Someone with the skills and the training to stalk his victims for extended periods."

"Why extended?" Bennet said. "Who's to say he didn't just follow them that one time?"

No, that didn't feel right to Maya at all. In fact, just following them didn't sound like enough. She returned to her desk and kept looking through Cynthia's file.

"Following might have worked for Jenette, but Cynthia?"

"What's different about her case?" Collingwood asked.

120

"That was definitely an ambush. It also explains why there was no sign of him on any cameras. This is someone who watched them for days, maybe longer. He got to know every facet of their lives."

"So stalking them, waiting for his opportunity?" Bennet suggested. She leaned over the desk, looking at the file as well, obviously trying to see what Maya saw.

Maya shook her head. "That's not this killer. He's not an opportunist, he's a planner. He had to set this up. For Jenette, that was easy enough: she always took the same shortcut, and it happened to be a spot he could use. That doesn't work for Cynthia, though. The place where she was killed *wasn't* somewhere she went past regularly."

"So how did he know that she would go there?" Collingwood asked, obviously starting to get it.

"The only way would be if he bugged them or tapped their phones. Otherwise, he would never have found out where Cynthia was going for dinner that night. He listened in to her conversations, found out where she would be on the night of the full moon, and used it to kill her."

The two detectives looked faintly impressed.

"So how do you get from that to a killer?" Bennet asked. "It tells us something about the guy, but doesn't lead us to a particular suspect. Jenette Hiatt worked with plenty of audio engineers who might have had the skills to plant a bug."

"Maybe, maybe not," Maya said. "It's a specialist skill. FBI technicians train for a long time to be able to do it well. You must have used listening equipment on stakeouts. Think about it, what did it take to get everything in place?"

"All right," Bennet admitted. "So you're looking for someone with particular skills."

Maya nodded and kept looking through Cynthia's file.

"What are you looking for?" Collingwood asked.

"I'm trying to find the contact details for the friend Cynthia Yoo was going to meet the night of her death. I think I have a way to get an answer to all of this."

*

Maya deliberately met Natasha Kalmar at the same restaurant she and Cynthia had been heading to. She wanted to put her in the same environment, wanted to jog any memories she could.

Besides, any answers she got relating to Cynthia were likely to be in Albany. Maya wanted to be ready to track them down.

"I haven't been here since... you know," Natasha said. She was a woman in her thirties, tall, with a severe expression and sharp features. Her clothes were expensive, her handbag Louis Vuitton. "When you called and suggested here, I almost turned you down."

"I'm glad you didn't," Maya said.

The restaurant around them was starting to get busy, with people starting to drift in for the earliest reservations. If Maya was wrong about all this and had to drive back to Corvallis, she was wasting time that she didn't have. Yet every instinct told her that this was where she needed to be. She suspected that she wouldn't get answers otherwise.

The restaurant's décor was simple, modern and upmarket, in a mix of grays, dark blues, and sudden splashes of white. The tables looked like reclaimed timber, and the wait staff flitted between tables, carrying dishes that looked far fancier than anything Maya would normally have eaten.

Briefly, she found herself thinking of her disastrous date with Marco. For the second time in a few days, she was in a nice restaurant, and again, it was going to be all about her work. This time, though, there was a chance that it might actually help things.

"What did you invite me here to ask, Agent?" Natasha asked, as she looked over a menu. Maya got the feeling that it was as much to hide her feelings about being here as it was to actually pick out something to eat.

"I need to ask you about Cynthia. The two of you were friends, right?"

"That's correct. We were in college at the same time, although I studied law while she went into medicine. We both went into our careers and did well, but... well, it was nice to have someone to meet up with from time to time and talk about things, just have fun."

A career in the law probably explained some of the cautiousness Natasha seemed to be exhibiting towards her. Lawyers generally didn't like being questioned.

"How often did you meet up like this?" Maya asked.

Natasha shrugged. "It varied. Sometimes every week, sometimes every month. There were a couple of spots in her divorce where all we would do was meet up for coffee. That was more often, I suppose. Why do you ask?"

"I'm trying to establish whether someone could have worked out that she was coming here based on just her routine," Maya said. "Was it always this restaurant?"

"Usually," Natasha said. "But not always. We were always on the lookout for new places."

"And did you tell many people about the places you were going? Who knew you were coming here?" Maya asked. Again, she had to eliminate the possibility that someone had found out that Cynthia was coming here through some other means.

"Why would we tell people?" Natasha said. "This was supposed to be time *away* from all the pressures of work. If people knew where to find us, then there would always be some last-minute thing that they needed us to look at. No, we would call one another to arrange it, maybe put it in our calendars, but that would be it."

Maya could feel her sense of hope building around her hunch.

"Natasha, do you know if Cynthia ever had dealings with someone who worked in audio surveillance? Did she mention any patients who worked in it, or maybe other friends?"

"There's a rather simple answer to that, Agent," Natasha said. "Cynthia was always very careful not to use names when it came to her patients, as I didn't use them when talking about my clients. It freed us up to talk about things that would be confidential, while keeping everything nice and anonymous. In any case, I don't think she mentioned a patient who did that sort of thing."

Maya could feel her sense of hope starting to fade now. Had she really wasted her time here, on her last day of this case?

"Although, now I think of it, there might be *one* person you could try," Natasha said, reigniting the embers of Maya's hope again.

"Who?"

"When she was getting divorced, we would talk through the details. Of course, I couldn't actually take on the work, because I'm more corporate consulting than that sort of thing, but I did recommend a very good divorce lawyer."

"And?" Maya said.

"And Cynthia hired a private investigator in the course of it. Ghastly little man, but very good at his job, apparently. Got all the pictures, and sound recordings, she needed to prove that her husband was having an affair. It saved her a fortune."

That sounded to Maya like the sort of person who would be more than capable of the sort of surveillance involved. If he thought that there was a problem with payment, if he was dissatisfied with the way things had happened, maybe that had been enough to push him to kill.

Could there have been a connection to Jenette as well, though? It seemed more than possible that someone like her, who liked knowing other people's secrets to bully them with, might go to that kind of length to find them out.

It was slender, but right then, it was the only potential lead Maya had.

"Do you remember the name of the PI?" she asked.

"Of course, I remember," Natasha said. "Benny Gibbs."

CHAPTER TWENTY FOUR

Down in the place the masked man had brought them all, Katya was more afraid than she had ever been in her life. More afraid than when she came out to her conservative parents. More afraid than when she'd given up on business school to pursue her dream of being a journalist. More afraid even than the moment when he'd grabbed her, dragging her here.

Everyone was afraid, down here. Katya knew some of them by now, because he let them out of their cages during the day to walk the limited space of the bunker he'd created. There were a few corridors, and the rows of "hutches" as he called them, but mostly they congregated in the large central chamber where he kept a chair that was more like a throne around which they had to gather while waiting for his pronouncements about what would happen to them. Some of them talked. Katya knew the names of a few: Sophie, Mai, Fleur. There was nothing to do but talk down here, even if the sense that *he* was always watching made it harder.

Today, almost no one was talking. A big part of that was what had happened to Carmel. He'd caught her trying to escape, and he'd killed her. Then he'd left her body in between their cages for an hour or more as a reminder of the price of disobedience. The sight of that had been enough to stun them all into silence for a while.

That was a part of the fear, and another part was that today was the day. Another of his deadlines, when one of them would disappear from their prison home. He said that he was releasing them because this FBI agent of his, Maya, was playing his game well.

Katya didn't believe it, not really. She didn't believe that a man like that would ever actually let them go. He would pretend it, and he would kill them. That was simply how men like him were.

And that made the fear a crushing, all-consuming thing for her, because *she* was the one that he had picked out for today. She was the one he had said he would release if Agent Gray did her job.

She was the one he was going to kill.

There wasn't a timer proclaiming the exact moment, this time. That made it worse, somehow, not better, because Katya didn't even know when the moment would come.

The worst part was not being able to do anything about it. Katya couldn't run, couldn't fight, couldn't hide. It was like being told that you had a terminal illness, that there was nothing they could do, that they were very sorry, as if that meant anything.

What was she meant to do with her last few hours on earth? Pray? Her father had been big on praying, but he'd never quite managed to beat the habit into her, or the bad out, as he put it. Reflect on her life? The problem was that Katya had only just been starting her *real* life when she'd been taken.

She didn't want to die.

All she could do was crouch there, hunched against a wall, avoiding eye contact with the others. There was nothing that they could say or do that would make any of this better. They couldn't save her. Even if they all teamed up and tried to take him down when he came, he would be ready for it. He would use that stun gun of his, the way he had in the past. If he saw them getting ready for an ambush, he might even bring in a real gun, and just kill them all outright.

Katya found herself sinking deeper and deeper into her fear, until she was a tight ball of it, barely concentrating on the rest of the large central chamber.

Even so, she noticed when the one who almost never talked walked over to her. It was kind of hard to miss her, after the beating their captor had given her. He'd done it in front of the rest of them, as if *they* were the ones who needed to learn the lesson, rather than the FBI who had angered him by trying to find him.

She came over, limping slightly, and sat down next to Katya. The sheer strangeness of it when she never normally spoke to anyone was enough to make Katya look over at her.

"My name is Megan," she said. "You're Katya, right?"

Katya nodded.

"And you think that you're going to die, don't you?"

Katya shrugged. That was far too close to the truth for Katya to admit to, even in a moment like this.

Megan reached out and put a hand on her shoulder. "Listen to me, you aren't going to die."

"You think he's actually going to release me?" Katya said, unable to keep the bitterness out of her voice.

To her surprise, Megan nodded. She of all people should know just how cruel their captor was.

"I think he takes the idea of rules so seriously, he's going to do it. Besides, if he were just killing us, my sister wouldn't keep playing his game."

Katya frowned at that as the logic of it started to make sense to her. There was a note of hope in her now that hadn't been there before. She also found herself staring over at Megan in surprise.

"What do you mean 'your sister?'"

"Agent Maya Gray is my older sister," Megan said.

Again, Katya found herself only able to stare at her. "So do you know what all this is about? Do you know why this is happening?"

Megan shook her head. "I don't know any more than you do. Just that you're going to get out of here."

"What if your sister doesn't solve this in time?" Katya asked.

"She will," Megan assured her. "She'll solve this, and you'll get out of here. And when you do, I need you to do something for me. I need you to give her a message."

CHAPTER TWENTY FIVE

Maya found that the best thing about Benny Gibb being a PI was that it was easy to locate his business address. She found herself looking at his website on her phone, and every line of it screamed "sleazy PI" to her.

We provide discrete solutions to all your problems. Whether it's a legal dispute, a cheating ex, or you simply want to keep track of that significant other, we're able to help.

Keep track of a significant other? A man who openly boasted about helping people to stalk their partners sounded like exactly the sort of person she needed to talk to.

His office was on one of the upper floors of a run-down apartment block. Maya guessed that Benny had watched a few too many movies, because he'd actually paid out the money for the old school door with frosted glass and *B. Gibb, PI,* on it in gold lettering.

Maya got out her ID and checked that her gun was ready before she went in. If she really was about to talk to a killer, there was no telling how he might react to her. For now, though, Maya decided to keep things civil, and knocked.

"It's open!" a woman's voice called.

Maya went in and found herself facing a middle-aged woman in a dark dress and knitted cardigan, who was seated behind a computer set on a rickety looking desk. She was dark haired, with horn rimmed glasses and an expression that said she'd taken in every detail of Maya as soon as she entered the room.

The room itself was small and lined with shelves on which files and legal books sat. Another door suggested a route through to a main office.

"Can I help you? What is it you need? Husband cheating? Neighbors starting some kind of legal dispute?"

"I need to see Benny Gibb," Maya said.

"I'm his secretary, Gwendolyn. If you want to talk to Mr. Gibb, then I'm afraid you need to make an appointment."

Maya pulled out her ID, making sure that the secretary got a good look at it. "It's in connection with a case."

"Need the help of a good PI?" Gwendolyn asked, she sounded faintly amused by it.

"*Is* he a good PI?" Maya shot back. She wanted to know what kind of man she was dealing with.

"He gets results," Gwendolyn said, and that told Maya everything she needed to know about his methods.

Then again, getting results by whatever means necessary seemed to be her own MO at the moment. At least Maya had the excuse of trying to protect Megan, though.

"So, can I see him?" Maya said. She started to step towards the door to the main office. "It's urgent."

"I'm afraid Mr. Gibb isn't in right now," Gwendolyn said. There was still a slightly defensive tone to it.

"So where is he?" Maya asked.

"I'm not sure if I can provide that information. Client confidentiality-"

"Applies to lawyers, and their clients. Not to the whereabouts of a PI who might find himself in the middle of a murder investigation." Maya put a lot more force into that and saw the secretary blanch slightly at the mention of murder. "Tell me where he is, and if he's not still there when I get there, if you call him to warn him, it will be you I arrest for obstruction."

"He's on a case," Gwendolyn said, looking slightly panicked now. "I can give you the address."

*

Maya raced across Albany to the address that Gwendolyn had given her. It was supposedly the address of a client's daughter's boyfriend, which only made it clear to Maya exactly how complicated half the things the PI got up to were.

She had to hurry now, because it was starting to get dark. How much longer did she have? The Moonlight Killer had said the night of the full moon, but did he mean midnight this time, or some other time that night?

Was it that he just wanted Maya to get to the killer before he struck again? If so, was this address really the one for a case, or was he using

129

it as a way to spy on a potential victim? Maybe he wouldn't even be there, and this was his way of arranging an alibi of sorts?

Maya pulled up in her rental car, parking it around the corner from the address she'd been given and approaching on foot. She walked calmly and casually, not wanting to give any indication that she was out there looking for one person in particular.

The address itself was a large brownstone building with big bay windows, lit up in the places where the occupants were home. Maya's eyes weren't really on the building, though. Instead, she found herself scanning the street to work out where someone might be watching from. Where would *she* watch from?

Her eyes fell on a row of parked vehicles out in front of the building. In particular, Maya found herself looking at a beat-up old panel van, large enough that it would be easy to set up comfortably for a stake out. If she had to put her money on anything there, it would be that.

Taking care to make it all seem casual, Maya walked towards it. She had to force herself not to stare at the van, to make it seem as though she was just out for an evening stroll, or on her way back home from work. Anyone competent would watch out for the possibility of counter-surveillance, even if Benny Gibb wasn't working in the kind of high-pressure environment brought about by a military operation or an FBI investigation.

When Maya was just a few feet from the van, she took out her ID and her gun. Approaching a vehicle was always dangerous, and she didn't want to be caught by surprise if Gibb had a weapon of his own, waiting for her.

Maya took a breath. She knew she couldn't hesitate now. Leave it too long and Gibb would spot that she was there. She tried the handle of the van's main door. To her surprise, it was unlocked, but maybe the alarm activated when it was locked, and Gibb didn't want to risk attracting attention.

Maya wrenched it open. Inside, the van was outfitted with an array of equipment that was faintly reminiscent of an FBI mobile command center, if one of those had been pieced together from equipment bought as cheaply as possible over the internet. There were a couple of screens showing camera footage, while crucially, Maya could hear low feeds from what seemed to be audio microphones or bugs playing in the background.

Benny Gibb sat on a swivel chair at the heart of it all. He was a weaselly looking little man in his late forties, with thinning dark hair, wearing a dark turtleneck sweater and black cargo pants. Maya suspected that he was going for the effect of invisibility against the darkness outside.

He turned around to face her as Maya pulled the door open. "Who the hell are you, and what do you think you're doing in my van?"

"Agent Gray, FBI," Maya said.

She saw Gibb's eyes go wide.

"I… you can't be…"

He threw himself forward, and Maya had to fight the instinct to shoot on reflex. She'd seen no sign of a weapon, and she wasn't going to shoot an unarmed man. That hesitation cost her, though, because it meant that Gibb slammed into her, and the impact knocked Maya back for a moment.

In that instant, he was off and running, sprinting into the dark.

Maya scrambled to her feet and set off after him. Gibb was quick, but Maya was determined to keep pace, not letting him out of her sight when his clothing and greater knowledge of the city would make it far too easy for him to hide.

Her feet thudded along the pavement, skidding slightly as she turned a corner after Gibb. He was still ahead, glancing back from time to time with fear on his face, as if Maya were trying to kill him rather than just catch up to him.

One thing was for certain: if he was that determined to run the moment that he heard Maya was FBI, then he had *something* to feel guilty about. Combined with what she'd seen in his van, she was starting to think that she might actually have found her man.

It was enough to spur her on to greater speed, determined to catch up to Gibb as he ran.

There was a busy street ahead, at least by the standards of a smaller city like Albany, with traffic flowing both ways, so that Maya felt sure that she would catch up to Gibb as he either stopped short of it or took a turn to try to find a new direction to run in.

Instead, he plunged out into it, dodging between the moving cars. Was he so desperate that he would rather risk dying than be caught? Maya saw a Chevrolet barely miss him, saw him stop and start and stop again as he tried to get across four lanes of traffic.

The real question was how desperate Maya was to catch him. She knew that the safe thing, the sensible thing, would be to hold back and cross where it was safe, then try to pick him up again somewhere on the far side. She should call it in and put police ahead of him.

The trouble with that strategy was that there was always a chance that he could get away. On another night, that wouldn't have mattered: they would simply have put out an APB for Gibb and picked him up within a couple of days. Now, Maya didn't have enough time left to risk it. Not with her sister's life on the line.

Trying to pick her moment, she plunged out into traffic in pursuit of her suspect.

Almost immediately, she had to pull back, as a big pickup truck only missed her by inches. Maya dove forward in its wake, heard the honking of a horn and the screech of brakes, but didn't stop.

She felt the wind as a car passed by behind her, froze in place to let another couple pass by, and tried to pick her next gap. Ahead of her, Gibb seemed to be doing the same, hesitating, looking back at her and then at the last lane of traffic.

Maya found the gap she was looking for and ran forward again. Again, she managed to avoid being run over by a fraction of a second, but this time she didn't stop. There was another gap, and she plunged into it, hoping that she'd judged it right.

As she did it, Gibb glanced around at her and obviously saw her coming, because he plunged forward, taking his last opportunity to get free.

Maya cursed and threw herself forward once more, sidestepping to avoid a VW bug, then keeping going. She saw the moment when the edge of a sedan barely clipped Gibb, not hard enough to break anything, but still hard enough to send him sprawling.

Maya saw her opportunity and pounced. She sprang forward through the traffic, then leapt on him as he tried to get up off the sidewalk. Her weight sent him back down to his stomach, where Maya held on as he tried to buck and fight.

Catching one of his arms, Maya wrenched it behind his back. He still tried to hit out at her with the other, but after a few seconds, Maya managed to catch that one too.

"Benny Gibb, you're under arrest."

132

CHAPTER TWENTY SIX

Maya sat in the interrogation room of the Linn County sheriff's department, trying to work out the best way to get through the wall of denial that was Benny Gibb. The PI sat opposite her in handcuffs, next to a lawyer who seemed almost as sleazy as he was, looking frightened and stubborn in equal measure. Sheriff O'Neil stood in the corner, too young looking to be a truly imposing presence, but with his eyes fixed firmly on Gibb.

Maya didn't rush to speak. Sometimes, silence could achieve more than any number of words.

"I didn't kill anyone!" Gibb said, out of nowhere.

"Didn't you?" Maya said. "We'll get to that. Technically, you're under arrest for fleeing a federal agent. You knew Cynthia Yoo, though, right?"

"She was a client of mine, that's all," Gibb replied. Maya could see the small beads of sweat starting to form on his face, the way his fingers entangled and disentangled nervously.

"She had you sneaking around after her husband?"

"'Sneaking' is a strong word."

But one that seemed to fit his job.

"Tell me, what was your relationship like with Cynthia?"

"She was my client. We didn't have a relationship."

That was defensive, perhaps a little too defensive, even given where they were. Gibb was nervous about something. Maya looked over at Sheriff O'Neil, giving him a small nod.

"I should tell you," he said, "that my deputies are currently searching your home for evidence. What do you think they're going to find?"

Maya saw the nervousness on Gibb's face tip over into outright fear, his complexion paling, his eyes starting to dart around as if looking for a way out.

"Cynthia was one of your clients. Was Jenette Hiatt?"

"Who?" His heart didn't seem to be in it, though.

"There's no point pretending that you haven't heard of her when I can see you have," Maya said. "She was murdered about a year ago, over in Corvallis, in exactly the same way as Cynthia Yoo."

"I've never met her," Gibb said. "Why would I know some bitch who worked in radio?"

"I never said that she worked in radio," Maya pointed out, picking Gibb up on his slip.

Gibb engaged in a hurried, whispered conversation with his lawyer.

"Ok, so it was in the news," Gibb shot back. "I saw when she died. It still doesn't mean that I had any kind of connection to her."

Everything about his body language said otherwise. Where before, he'd been glancing around in fear, now he was staring straight forward and holding himself perfectly still, as if afraid of giving anything away. The change in pattern meant something, Maya was sure of it.

"Does your work take you over to Corvallis often, Benny?" she asked.

"Sometimes. I go where people need me."

"You make it sound like such a public service," Sheriff O'Neil put in. "Spying on people, sneaking around after them."

"Finding out the truth," Gibb said. "If they don't have anything to hide, they've got nothing to worry about."

Maya gave him a level look. "You seem pretty worried right now, Benny. What do you have to hide? What did you do?"

Maya kept that level stare going, again giving Gibb silence to see if he would feel the need to fill it.

In that silence, Sheriff O'Neil's phone went off. He answered it.

"O'Neil here. What did you find? I see. Right. Got it. Ok, send me photographs of the relevant parts, then bring it all back here."

As he spoke, Maya saw Gibb getting more and more worried.

Maya waited for him to finish, stretching the moment out, before she asked the next question.

"What did Sheriff O'Neil's people find at your place, Benny?"

"It was all for work! All of it. I was just doing my job!"

Maya looked over at Sheriff O'Neil, who held out his phone.

"My deputies found photographs. Lots of photographs, all of women, all obviously taken with a long lens through windows. They've forwarded the most relevant ones."

134

Maya flicked through them, and instantly, she recognized the woman under Benny Gibb's lens. Jenette Hiatt was there, in her apartment, getting changed, walking around, taking a bath…

"I thought you said that you only knew *of* Jenette, Benny," Maya said, turning one of the most incriminating photographs towards him. "It looks to me as though you were trying to get to know about her pretty intimately."

"It's not what it looks like!" Gibb insisted.

Maya raised an eyebrow. Was he really going to keep up his protestations even then?

"Really? Because it looks as though you were stalking her, tracking her, *hunting* her. It looks as though you were doing surveillance prior to killing her."

Gibb looked panicked, rising half out of his seat. His lawyer put a hand on his arm, pushing him down. He clearly knew how bad it would look for his client if he tried to run again.

To be fair, though, it looked pretty bad now.

"Where were you on the nights that Cynthia Yoo and Jenette Hiatt were murdered?" Maya asked.

The lawyer chose that moment to speak up. "My client can hardly be asked to remember his whereabouts on two specific occasions so long ago."

With anyone else, Maya might have agreed. "I think Benny remembers perfectly. I think either he was stalking Jenette, and the news she was dead would have hit him like a hammer, or he did it, and he knows his alibi perfectly. Which is it, Benny?"

"I… I was out working," Benny said. "Gwendolyn, my secretary, will be able to confirm it."

Maya shook her head. "She'll be able to confirm that you weren't in the office. She'll be able to confirm that you said you were working, maybe even that you had a case, but she won't be able to confirm that you were there."

"I didn't kill them!" Gibb insisted. "I couldn't have! I loved Jenette!"

He meant it, that much was clear from every line of his face, but that didn't change anything for Maya.

"I loved her, and I wanted to be close to her, so yes, I followed her, and a few others. Maybe I got… a little obsessed."

"A little," Sheriff O'Neil said.

"But I could never hurt them," Gibb said. "I couldn't."

"You still haven't given me the details of where you were the night of Jenette's murder," Maya said.

"I… I'll write it down."

His lawyer passed him a pen and paper. Maya caught the faint tremble in his hand as he wrote, the way it took him a couple of attempts to grip the pen properly. It could have just been fear, but she wasn't sure.

"Here you go," he said. "You can check. I-"

Benny's lawyer put a hand on his arm. "I would like some time to confer with my client about this new evidence before he says anything else."

Maya thought about how little time there was left, thought about pushing the issue, but the fact was that, if she did that, there was a chance of the whole case being thrown out. Besides, they still had a few hours before the night was done. For the first time in three days, she had time.

"All right," Maya said. "We'll leave the two of you to talk."

She and Sheriff O'Neil headed out of the interrogation room together. As soon as the door shut behind them, he turned to her.

"It seems I owe you an apology. I thought you were just here chasing ghosts, but it seems like you've actually caught the guy who did this."

"I just want the truth," Maya said.

"We have more than enough to hold Gibb. If he has any sense, he'll start talking."

"In the meantime, we need to start checking Gibb's so-called alibi," Maya said. "If we can show that he wasn't where he claims, this gets a lot easier."

"I'll coordinate with the Corvallis PD and tell them what we have."

"Cooperating, Sheriff?"

She saw Sheriff O'Neil shrug. "I don't like that they turned their murder into some grand circus, like a serial killer is a tourist attraction. I didn't want any part of that, but I can still do my job."

He could do his, Maya would do hers, and with luck, they would get a confession out of Benny Gibb well before the Moonlight Killer's deadline.

*

136

He had given up on watching Agent Gray, but he still tuned in to the Albany police channels. It was important to keep track of them on a night like tonight. He didn't want any surprises.

That was how he knew that they'd brought in Benny Gibb for the murders of Jenette and Cynthia. That was both a relief and a worry. It was a relief because they'd arrested someone other than him.

It was a worry because it hit far too close to home. He knew Benny, after all. He'd been the one to show the budding detective how to perform surveillance, been the one to show him how useful audio monitoring could be in his cases. Benny had brought him in for what had been supposed to be just a couple of cases, but it had turned into six months of working with him, teaching him, helping him to set up his own equipment.

Even Benny's van was modelled after his, although his was adapted to his own needs, focusing more on sound, making sure that all of it could be routed through the headphones that let him hear the world around him.

If they found out too much from Benny, it could be a problem. Then again, if they really believed that he was their killer… that could give him all the time he needed to act.

He had to check, and that meant focusing his attentions on Maya Gray again. He drove around to the Linn County Sheriff's Department, picking a spot where he wouldn't be too conspicuous and setting to work with his microphones. Of course, it helped that he could listen in to Agent Gray's phone as well. It was as good as having a bug in the middle of the building.

Everything came in, channeled through his headphones. He didn't know what his life would be like without them. Actually, no, he could *remember* what his life had been like, and he had no wish to ever go back to it.

It had been awful, losing so much of his hearing that just to walk around in the every-day world, he had to wear sound amplifying headphones. Other people went for hearing aids, but at least with these he'd been able to hide it for a while, picking something that wouldn't be seen at the radio station.

That was before that bitch Jenette had found out. She'd spent her time mocking him, and he tried to tell himself that it had been the same as with everyone she met; but it *wasn't* the same, and he couldn't let it stand.

So he'd killed her. It had been easier than he'd thought it would be, just a matter of preparation really. Just a matter of being careful. He'd decided on copying the Moonlight Killer early on, because it seemed like an easy way to point the authorities in another direction, but he couldn't copy the whole MO. There was nowhere public enough that Jenette would be quickly so that he could also kill her without the risk of someone coming up that he didn't hear.

Cynthia had been almost as bad as Jenette. She hadn't mocked him, but she hadn't helped him either, when she obviously could have. She'd said that he wasn't a suitable candidate, like it was *his* fault that she couldn't fix his hearing.

By that point, after Jenette, it had been easier to kill her than not to.

Which left tonight, and Cindy.

She'd been the nurse who'd looked after him in the hospital, there by Dr. Yoo's side for some of it. She'd tried to tell him the lie that everything would be fine without his hearing, that he would be the same as before, but then she'd turned him down flat when he'd asked her to dinner. Everything about her had made it clear that she was disgusted with him just for asking, that he wasn't good enough, and never would be.

She deserved to die, along with the rest, and tonight would be the night.

CHAPTER TWENTY SEVEN

The full moon shone down on Maya as she stepped outside and tried to think. She wanted to feel satisfied, wanted to feel that all of this was done, and that it was only a matter of time until a woman would be released.

Yet something didn't add up. Two things, in fact.

The first was that while Benny Gibb had plenty of potential motive to kill Jenette Hiatt as her stalker, his connection to Cynthia didn't provide such a convenient reason for him to kill her. Maya had been hoping that when the local PD started to go through his home, they might find evidence of some feud between them, but as far as she could see now, Cynthia had been a perfectly satisfied client. Benny had done his job, however sleazy, and she'd gotten everything she wanted in the divorce.

Had she not paid him? Had they argued? No, her lawyer friend would have heard about anything like that and would already have told Maya.

The second thing that didn't add up was the shake in Benny's hand as he'd written down the details of his alibi.

Maya went back inside. Sheriff O'Neil looked pleased.

"We've got him. We've actually got the guy who killed Cynthia Yoo. I'll admit, I was a little worried when you showed up, going on about the Moonlight Killer, but this is impressive."

"There's something I still need to check," Maya said.

"We're going through his office now to try to find his motive for killing Cynthia, if that's it," Sheriff O'Neil said. "I know it's the weaker link in this, Agent Gray, but we'll find it. One missed payment, one photo of her that shouldn't be there, one suggestion of blackmail, and we'll have him."

He'd seen that part, at least, but not the whole of it.

"I still need to check," Maya said.

She walked back into the interrogation room, where it seemed that Gibb was still conferring with his lawyer. The lawyer looked up as Maya entered, and he clearly wasn't happy.

"What did you do to your hand, Benny?" Maya asked.

"Agent, I need privacy to speak with my client. Until I get that, he won't be answering any more of your questions."

"This might exonerate your client. What did you do to your hand, Benny?"

Gibb was silent for a few more seconds, then Maya saw him shrug. "I hurt it three years back when some boyfriend decided he didn't like me taking pictures. We got into a fight. I broke the hand. Hasn't been right since."

"Define 'not right' for me," Maya said.

Gibb looked a little annoyed at that. "What do you want me to say? That I can barely hold my camera anymore? That I have to have some stupid thing I bought off the shopping channel just to open jars? Are you just here to make me feel bad, Agent?"

Maya didn't mind making Gibb feel a little bad about his life, given that he was still a stalker who had obviously spent his time spying on Jenette Hiatt and other women.

He wasn't a murderer, though.

He couldn't be, not when he didn't have the grip strength to even hold a ligature, let alone strangle two women to death with it. He physically couldn't have committed the crimes that he had seemed such a promising suspect for.

A sinking feeling spread through Maya at the thought of how much time she'd spent chasing Gibb. She'd thrown everything she had at him, and it wasn't him. Already, outside, the full moon was high overhead.

Maya went outside to find Sheriff O'Neil.

"What was all that about?" he asked.

"I'm pretty sure that Gibb isn't the killer," Maya said.

"What? I've got guys going over his place. We'll find the proof."

"You'll find something circumstantial. You'll find a motive, and his alibi will be trash. Maybe it will even be enough to persuade a jury, but it's not *him*."

Sheriff O'Neill looked nonplussed by that. "Agent Gray, you can't chase a man, arrest him, and then suddenly decide that he's not a killer on a whim."

Maya shook her head. The sheriff had been doing such a good job of keeping up until now.

"Do you know how much effort it takes to strangle someone who's fighting for their life?" Maya said. "Can you imagine how much Cynthia Yoo would have thrashed around, trying to break free? Imagine if Benny Gibb were holding onto that ligature. Do you really see him keeping his grip?"

"Even so, I want to hold him," Sheriff O'Neil said.

"As a stalker, sure. As a murderer? It's not him, Sheriff."

"We'll see."

They would see, but probably by the time Sheriff O'Neil came around, Maya's window of opportunity to solve this case would be gone.

"You do that. I need to catch the real killer."

Maya walked outside, wishing that she had a plan to back it up. Benny Gibb had eaten up her time, and now, Maya didn't even have the thread of a lead to pull on.

The real killer was out there, probably getting ready to kill another woman, and there was nothing Maya could do about it.

She hated feeling that helpless, especially when she was pretty sure that the Moonlight Killer was out there listening in to all of this, judging everything she did.

Listening in.

Those words stuck in Maya's head, refusing to dislodge themselves. What did it matter that the Moonlight Killer listened in to her? Maya knew that, and she couldn't change it.

No, that wasn't the important part, was it? The important part was that he wasn't the only one who could listen in. Gibb had shown that, back in his van, and Maya had already *guessed* that the killer liked to use audio surveillance when it came to targeting his victims.

If he planned to kill tonight, then he might already be stalking his victim, listening to her every movement, following her life and picking it apart for weaknesses. He would already have his spot planned, but Maya guessed that he would want to be careful.

Especially if he knew that the FBI were in town, looking for him.

Would he know? That was the question, but the answer seemed obvious to Maya. She hadn't exactly been quiet about her investigation, and the chase with Benny Gibb had made it even more obvious that she was there. Maya imagined that the local cops would have talked about her too, trying to assess what this stranger was doing in their midst on the channels they kept to themselves.

The killer would know that she was there, and that would make him cautious. *More* cautious, because everything about the first two murders said that he was careful in the extreme about the possibility of being discovered.

He picked his sites so that no one would see him. He followed his targets so he could be sure of his opportunity. He mimicked the Moonlight Killer's whole MO so that it would deflect attention.

Was it such a big leap to assume that the killer would listen in to her and the police on the night when he was due to kill again?

Maya didn't think so. In fact, she thought that it was almost impossible that he *wouldn't* be listening.

The only question now was how she could use that fact. If he'd been listening in for the last few minutes, then he would have heard that Maya didn't have any answers, that she'd had to admit that she'd arrested the wrong man.

What he *wouldn't* have heard her say aloud, though, was that she had no clue where to look for him. If he was watching and listening, could she make use of that fact?

Maya stood there, trying to work it all through. It would be difficult, and possibly dangerous. She would have to do this alone, because if she tried to explain her plan to the sheriff or his deputies, there was a chance that the killer would hear every word of it. More than that, the sheriff would probably try to talk her out of it, and Maya didn't have enough time for that.

She didn't have any time now for anything, except one last shot at catching the killer.

Taking out her phone, Maya called Harris.

"Gray," he said. "You'd better be calling to tell me that you've caught the killer."

Maya had to stop herself from reacting to that. Her boss had already made it clear how much rested on her finding the killer in time. She couldn't afford to be distracted by that right now, though. She had to focus on the case, and on finding the man who had actually done all this. This phone call was a necessary part of it, no matter how awkward it was.

"We pulled a guy in," Maya said. "Benny Gibb, a PI connected to both Jenette Hiatt and another victim of the same killer."

"Sounds promising," Harris said, some of the gruffness going out of his voice.

"At the time he seemed like a pretty good suspect, but now it's obvious that there's no way it could have been him."

There was a pause at the other end of the line. "You're calling me to tell me that you *don't* have the killer?"

"I'm calling to let you know that I know who the real killer is, sir." This was the difficult part of it.

"Who?"

"After everything with Benny Gibb, I hope you'll understand if I want to wrap this up neatly before I present it all to you," Maya said. It was a fine line, trying to find something that both her boss and the listening killer would understand and accept.

"Not confident that you have the right guy?" Harris said. He obviously wasn't going to let this go.

"I'm confident, but we both know that if I just tell you, Reyes will jump in and try to steal all the glory."

There was no way that he actually could from this distance, but after everything that had happened in the last few weeks, it made for a convenient excuse.

Maya heard Harris grunt. "Whatever. Just so long as you catch the guy. You *are* going to catch him?"

This was the moment that counted, the one that could make or break this case. Maya knew that she had to get this right. One sentence could catch a killer or set him free to kill again.

"I'm going to. I know who he is, and I know where he's going to be tonight. Actually, I need to go, sir. I need to get there before he does if I'm going to catch him."

"Understood," Harris said. Maya just hoped that the killer got her message as well. "Good luck out there."

Maya hoped that she wouldn't need luck.

She hung up and headed to her rental car. She got her tactical vest out and put it on. If the killer was watching, then it was nothing he wouldn't expect. She got in behind the wheel and made sure that her gun was ready too. There was always a risk here that the killer would decide to take her out in order to free up his path to his victim. After all, he knew now that Maya was doing this alone.

Alone, against a killer who had already murdered two people. Maya believed that she was prepared for this, but even so, she could think of a dozen ways that it could all go wrong. If it did, it wasn't just her life on the line, but her sister's too. She had to make this work.

Maya pulled out of the sheriff's station, driving smoothly and keeping her eyes on her mirrors. She'd had plenty of counter surveillance training before now. Against a truly skilled team, it was hard to spot a tail, because they leapfrogged vehicles or just used satellite or drone imagery.

The killer wasn't working with a skilled surveillance team, though. That meant he had to do this the old-fashioned way.

When Maya saw headlights flick on and a van pull into traffic behind her, she knew she had her man.

CHAPTER TWENTY EIGHT

He'd thought that he was safe.

He had to ignore his panic as he slid his van into traffic behind Agent Gray's car, following a couple of cars behind so that it wouldn't be obvious that he was tailing her. He'd had a lot of practice following people.

He'd been so confident when Agent Gray had decided that Benny Gibb was the killer. He'd been certain that his old acquaintance would take the fall. He'd thought that he would be able to act with impunity tonight. Now, he was more uncertain than he'd been since he began all of this, not knowing what he was meant to do next.

He took a turn after Agent Gray, barely resisting the urge to accelerate to keep up with her. That was a surefire way to draw attention to himself, and if there was one thing he didn't want to do right now, it was draw any attention.

Somehow, though, he had. Somehow, she'd worked out that it was him. He'd spent so long planning all of this exactly so that no one would be able to work out that it was him.

He forced himself to be patient, pulling around the corner slowly, catching sight of Agent Gray's car again and continuing to follow. He pulled around another car, slid into the space beyond it, and kept going.

She couldn't know. He told himself that again and again as he drove, a sense of panic welling up in him. She couldn't. He'd been so careful, left no traces for anyone to follow. He'd been a ghost.

And yet somehow, she'd found out where he was going to be tonight. He'd heard her say as much to her boss. She'd found out who he was, and where he was going. She was going to interfere.

She was the only one who knew. That had been clear from the phone call too. As they both pulled up behind a red light, he considered his options. Would it be beyond the realms of possibility to run her car off the road? To find a quiet spot and kill her for getting in the way? To clear the way for one murder with another?

No, he knew the foolishness of that. A murder was something that needed to be planned carefully. He needed to arrange it, pick his moment, ensure that he wouldn't be seen. Killing an FBI agent was something that would attract attention, not deflect it. It would bring more of them swarming, and then they *might* find him.

It was something only to be done in the direst situation. Of course, if she really did know where he was going, then he might have no choice.

He kept following, down through Albany. This wasn't the route he'd been planning to take tonight, but that didn't mean anything. The agent could be taking a circuitous route for a reason, maybe stopping to gather some piece of evidence.

Perhaps the best thing to do was to go home and try this another night. If it came to it, would he back down? Would he abandon his kill for tonight? No, he couldn't. He had to do this. If Agent Gray truly knew who he was, then there would be no second chances. If he backed off, then she would just come for him in the morning, and his chance would be gone completely.

There was more to it than that, though. Cindy *deserved* to die, and it had to be tonight. He'd put too much effort into this to give it up now. He wasn't going to sit back and plan the whole thing again. He wasn't going to let her mess up his life again, just by going on living.

No, he would do this, whatever it took, but it was still best to see if Agent Gray really was going to be a problem in all of this, or not.

She drove, and he tried to tell himself that there was no way that she might know who he was. That this was a bluff. It was looking more and more like one the further they drove.

She actually drove to a local park, pulling into the parking lot and sliding her car into a space between a minivan and an Escalade.

He almost laughed with relief. She thought that he was going to strike *here*? She thought this was the place where he was going to kill Cindy? That was ludicrous, not even close to being the right answer.

He felt his panic subsiding. He was safe after all. Agent Gray *had* been bluffing, or she was just plain wrong. She'd gone with something that made sense based on the places he'd left the bodies, so now she was going to sit here waiting while he was nowhere near here.

That was fine by him. She could sit here all night. Meanwhile, he had a murder to commit. Slowly, without stopping, he drove on.

*

Maya sat in the parking lot of the park, trying not to be too obvious as she used her mirrors to check for the van that was following her. If the driver caught her looking around, then he would quickly guess what she was doing, and this would turn into either a chase or a fight.

Maya couldn't afford either of those things, not yet. Not when the driver could turn around and say that he had no idea what she was talking about, when he could just walk away and pretend innocence.

Maya had to catch him in the act. She had to *prove* this.

That meant continuing to sit there, waiting for the van to drive past. Maya could see that it was a silver Chevy Express, far too similar to Benny Gibb's choice of van for it to be a coincidence. She would have to ask him about that later, but now wasn't the moment to do anything except try to stop a killer.

The first step was letting him go, watching as he turned back towards the entrance to the park. Maya had to force herself to wait, letting her target get a reasonable distance ahead before she put her car into gear and pulled off.

Now it was time to see if she could follow him better than he'd followed her.

Maya pulled left out of the park, following well behind, using the traffic of the city to shield her car from view. One good thing about a rental car like this was that it was a lot less distinctive than a van, a lot harder to make out at a distance, in the dark.

She cut her main headlights, just to be sure. On the city streets, she could see well enough by the streetlights, and it meant that the van's driver wasn't going to have the flash of headlights in his mirrors telling him that he had a tail, the way she'd had.

Maya wished that she had a team with her right then. She'd been so cocky about spotting a tail forced to do things the old-fashioned way, but now, here she was, forced into exactly the same situation. She could do nothing except stay far enough back to keep out of sight, following the van's turns, trying to get a sense of where it was going.

The only problem with that was that Maya didn't know the city well enough to guess. If this had been D.C., maybe she could have worked out where the driver was going and been there waiting when he got there. As it was, she could only take turns as he did, following along, trying to make sure that she didn't lose touch.

The van joined a stream of traffic, and Maya flicked her headlights on for this part. The last thing she needed was a driver hitting his horn because she was driving along without them, drawing attention to her. Or worse, some cop pulling her over for it.

At least here, among the other cars, she didn't stand out. She could lurk there, flowing along a few cars behind the van, making sure that its driver never had a chance to spot her.

Who was he, and where was he planning to go for his final kill? Did even the Moonlight Killer know that part, or had he simply sent her here knowing that there would *be* a murder tonight? Presumably, not even he knew everything about the cases.

Maya certainly didn't know who this was. Maybe there was some way to work it out by trawling through the case files, tracking down everyone with a link to Cynthia Yoo and Jenette Hiatt, taking weeks over the interviews until she found an answer that way. But to find anything tonight, this was her only hope, just follow and try to make sure that she was there in time to stop whoever this was from killing again.

Should she call for backup? If so, how? For all Maya knew, the killer was still listening in to her every word. If she came out and just told a dispatcher what was happening, then he would take off, disappear, or play innocent.

No, she needed to be smarter than that. She needed to call backup, without it being too obvious.

Maya used her phone to punch through to a dispatcher.

"Dispatch."

"This is Agent Maya Gray with the FBI. I need backup standing by for me."

"What's your situation, Agent?" the dispatcher asked.

"I have found the location where I believe a murder is about to be committed. The killer of Jenette Hiatt and Cynthia Yoo is going to be there."

"Understood," the dispatcher said. "What's the location?"

"I'll send that once I'm certain he's here," Maya said. "I don't want to spook him. I just need cars on standby, ready to come quickly when I call."

"We'll be ready, Agent," the dispatcher promised.

It was the most Maya could do without alerting the killer. For now, she had to just keep him in sight, keep following.

To keep from being too obvious, the next time the van turned off, Maya kept going for another street, then took a turning in the same direction. She accelerated slightly, playing catch up. Looking over to her left at the intersections she passed. Under the streetlights, she caught sight of the van there, moving along without any sign that the driver had spotted her. It meant that there was no chance that the driver would look around and see her car.

In a perfect world, Maya would have darted back into traffic, getting ahead of the van and trying to tail it from in front, but that was something that only worked when the target wasn't watching for a particular car. She had to keep things simple, turning back into the same street as the van, wanting to slide in behind it once again.

Maya was almost there when a large Pontiac cut in front of her at a set of lights, horn blaring as it changed lanes without warning. Maya had to slam her foot on the brake to keep from hitting it, and she felt the jolt of the car coming to a halt. The lights were red now, and Maya wanted to just shoot across the junction, but with the speed cars were flashing past, there was no chance of doing it without being t-boned and probably killed.

Instead, she had to wait for the lights to change, then hurry across the junction, speeding past the Pontiac in an effort to catch sight of the van again.

Maya's heart felt as though it were made of lead. The shock of disappointment flooded through her, quickly followed by the fear of what might happen next. She'd lost the van, with no sign of it ahead of her.

The killer was on his way to commit another murder, and she couldn't stop him if she wasn't there.

That was a terrifying thought in itself; but worse than that, if Maya couldn't find the killer again, her sister was going to die.

She had to find that van.

CHAPTER TWENTY NINE

Maya cursed and sped up, trying not to panic and failing. She'd lost the van. She'd lost the *killer*. She'd lost him, right at the point when she needed to stop him.

She skidded past a pickup, then cut in front of a Prius, ignoring it as the driver hit their horn. The time for being careful was past. Maya needed to catch sight of it again, or both her sister and another woman were dead.

If she'd gotten the van's license plate, all of this would be easier. She could call in for traffic cam recognition on the number, because at this point, it mattered far less if the killer heard that she was coming, so long as she found him in time.

Maya scanned the streets she passed, trying to see if he'd taken a turn that Maya didn't see. She couldn't spot him ahead, so it made sense that he must have turned off somewhere. But where?

Spotting a single van down a side street would have been hard enough in daylight, but by night, trying to pick it out under the streetlights, it was nearly impossible. Maya found herself staring so intently that when she glanced up, she had to jerk the wheel hard to avoid rear-ending a bus.

Maya swerved past it and kept looking. She was getting towards smaller streets, and now she had to drive a little slower to give herself enough time to look at each one.

It was no use. There was no sign of the van in any of the streets and picking it out as she was passing was likely to be next to impossible. She needed another option. It wasn't enough to just chase around hoping to get lucky; she needed to *think*. Where would the killer be going? Where would his victim be?

For a moment or two, it seemed like an impossible question. The killer could be driving anywhere. Maya might already have driven past wherever he'd taken his van without spotting it.

That thought was a terrifying one, and almost enough to make her turn back, wanting to go over the streets she'd passed again and check each one carefully. That would take forever, though, and in that time, the killer could easily murder his victim.

Then Maya saw the small hospital down one of the side streets, and she knew in an instant that was where the killer had to be heading.

It made sense, didn't it? Jenette Hiatt had been a bully, so she could have provoked *anyone* into killing her; but Cynthia Yoo? Maya was convinced that her death had to do with her job. If someone was upset with her over something relating to medical care, maybe that same person wanted to target another medical professional?

Maya knew that it was a hunch at best, but right then, it was all that she had to go on. That instinct she had was based on the little that she knew about the killer from his crimes and, as she thought about it, another small piece of the puzzle fell into place for her:

The killer had some kind of hearing loss.

It explained the focus on audio surveillance, along with maybe both the connection to Cynthia and Jenette. It potentially explained a *lot*. Assuming it was true. Maya knew that she was assuming a lot, betting lives on her hunch, but she simply didn't have anything better.

Accelerating again, she drove towards the hospital, heading for its parking lot.

When Maya got inside, for a moment or two, she thought she'd misjudged it. She couldn't see the van, and disappointment flared through her, making her feel as though she'd lost everything. She'd bet everything on a hunch, and it hadn't paid off. Now the killer was even further ahead, with Maya's chances of stopping him receding by the moment.

Then she saw it, half hidden behind an F100 pickup. The silver of the van she'd been looking for sat there. Maya drove past, pulling into a space just a little further along, then got out of her car.

She pulled her Glock, ready for the possibility that she might be confronting a killer in the next few seconds. Maya used the surrounding cars for cover, not knowing if the killer had spotted her arriving. She padded forward on silent feet, approaching the rear of the van. Carefully, one handed, she reached out for the doors and tested them. Unlike Benny Gibb's van, the doors here were locked. Maya kept creeping around the side of it, making her way to the driver's side window with her heart pounding in anticipation. She made the final step, levelling her gun at the windshield.

The van was empty.

151

No, not empty. It was probably full of evidence relating to the crimes. At the very least, if this killer was like Benny Gibb, then he would have all of his surveillance equipment there, complete with records of everyone he'd looked at. The killer wasn't there, though, which meant what? That he'd already moved on into the building? That he was already stalking his victim, ready to kill her?

Maya knew that there was no time left to lose. The van could wait, but the killer couldn't.

Where was he? Maya checked the quiet spaces around the parking lot, but there was no sign of anyone waiting there. Had the killer picked out a spot where he could ambush his victim inside the hospital instead? Was that even possible?

Maya ran for the entrance to the hospital. A security guard there moved to intercept her, but Maya already had her ID out.

"I'm in pursuit of a dangerous killer," Maya said. "Has anyone suspicious gone through here in the last couple of minutes?"

The security guard shook his head. Maya understood. This killer wasn't someone who was going to stand out. He was someone who blended in, who moved silently and disappeared without a trace. He wasn't someone a security guard was going to spot and intercept.

She moved to the front desk of the hospital instead, pushing past the people waiting for treatment and setting her ID down on the counter. The receptionist there stared at her in shock, looked down at the ID, and then stared at her again.

"How can I help you, Agent?" the receptionist said.

Maya tried to think. There was no way that the receptionist had spotted the killer if the security guard hadn't. He wasn't someone who stood out.

He didn't stand out, so why was he walking into the middle of a crowded hospital? He couldn't just murder someone openly here. He couldn't walk up to someone here and murder her, hoping to get away with it.

That wasn't how it worked. It wasn't how *he* worked. With both of the previous two murders, he'd killed in a deliberately quiet spot before moving the body to a more public location.

Maya understood why now, too. If he had some kind of hearing impairment, then he wouldn't be able to hear potential threats coming. He *had* to kill in deserted locations, when the real Moonlight Killer could take his opportunities wherever he found them.

In a hospital, there wouldn't be opportunities to strike just waiting. The killer would have planned his moment, which meant that there was a reason he was here *now*, at this particular time.

"Are there any departments where a shift changeover is taking place?" Maya asked.

It was the only solution. It had to be. The killer had picked this moment because he knew his victim would be alone, and in a busy hospital, the best time to manage that, possibly the *only* time to manage that, was as his victim came off shift and made her way to her car.

"I don't know, I'd have to check," the receptionist said.

"Then check," Maya said. "But hurry. Someone's life is in danger."

"Ok, so there are a few. Physical therapy, cardiology…"

"What about audiology?" Maya asked. It was the department that made the most sense, if the killer was targeting someone who had wronged him along with Cynthia Yoo.

"Yes, they're on the list, but-"

"Which way?" Maya demanded.

"It's on the second floor."

"Ok," Maya said. She turned to run for the nearest stairwell, then thought better of it. She needed to do this properly. She turned back to the receptionist. "Get your security to lock down the hospital. There is a killer loose in your building. Call the local PD and tell them that Agent Maya Gray of the FBI needs her backup to this location. They'll know what you mean."

There, Maya had done what she could to make sure that the killer wouldn't get free. She didn't think that he posed a threat to the ordinary civilians in the hospital, but there was no way of knowing that for sure, and Maya didn't want to risk it. When the Linn County Sheriff Department arrived, they would secure the building.

For now, though, she had a killer to catch.

Maya sprinted for the stairs, dodging out of the way of a patient being taken through to a treatment room, then taking the stairs two at a time until she reached the second floor. The only advantage she might have was that the killer would be taking things cautiously, moving at a pace that wouldn't attract attention. Maya didn't have to worry about that.

She got to the second floor, followed the signs for audiology, and quickly found herself in a seemingly empty department. It was as though the whole place was a ghost ship, abandoned and pristine. Maya

153

stood in the middle of an empty waiting area, with doors leading off to treatment rooms, and she might have been the only person in the world right then.

It only occurred to her then that, for a department like this, there was no reason to run through the night. It didn't have inpatients, so it would shut down and then open again in the morning. Everyone was gone, and Maya didn't know where they'd gone, or where the killer might have decided to strike.

"Hello?" she called out. "Is anyone still here?"

"Hello?" a voice called back. A woman in a nurse's uniform emerged from a side door. "I'm sorry, we're closing up for the night. I'm the last one here."

Was *this* the killer's target?

Maya knew that there was no time to waste. "My name is Agent Gray. I'm with the FBI. I believe that there's a killer coming to target someone in your department. Do you have any connection with a doctor over at the medical center across town named Cynthia Yoo?"

"Dr. Yoo? The one who was murdered?"

"That's her," Maya said. "Do you have any connection with her? Have you ever worked with her? Do you have the same patients?"

"I've never worked with her," the nurse said. "But Cindy did. She says Dr. Yoo was a pioneer. She only moved here after the doctor died, because she said she couldn't stand working in the same place after that."

That sounded like exactly the kind of person the killer might target.

"Where is Cindy now?" Maya asked.

"She left only a few minutes ago," the nurse said. "I guess she'll be heading back to her car."

Maya started to turn towards the door to the audiology department.

"Not that way," the nurse said. "The parking lot out front is for patients. They make all of *us* park out back, then they get annoyed with us when we cut through the new wing they're building to get there, rather than walking all the way around."

"What new wing?" Maya asked.

"A whole new set of departments," the nurse said. "They've been building it for months. Cindy always cuts through it on her way back. It's always deserted at this time of night."

An empty construction site sounded like exactly the kind of place where the killer might strike. It was a spot where no one would see him make his kill, and that he could enter or leave easily. It was perfect.

"Which way?" Maya demanded.

The nurse pointed. "Through those doors, then down to your right until you find the doors with the plastic over them to keep the construction dust in. You can't miss it."

Maya hoped not, because a woman's life was in danger. With her gun clutched in her hand, she set off at a run, hoping that she would get to the killer in time.

CHAPTER THIRTY

Maya crept through the half-built section of the hospital, gun held ahead of her, feeling the tension rise with every step. She picked her way around piles of building materials and between boxed up machinery, trying desperately not to make a sound.

This was it. The killer was here somewhere, probably only a little way ahead of her, already stalking his victim. Maya found herself caught between the need to move quietly to avoid the killer hearing her coming and the need to move quickly so that she would make it in time.

The unfinished wing added to the tension of it all with its strangeness. Parts of it seemed almost ready to be opened, with whole rooms set up with medical equipment standing ready, only needing patients to walk into them. Other sections were little more than a skeleton of the place, with timber frames and pipes waiting for drywall over the top.

Plastic sheeting was everywhere. It covered large sections of the floor to catch dust and hung down across open sections to prevent it spreading as any contractors worked. There were lights on in some spots where they'd been installed, obviously connected to the rest of the hospital's systems, but other places were dark, not yet hooked up.

The result was a confusing maze of half-light, with the plastic distorting everything. Maya had to pick her way through it, trying to find her suspect, trying to get to Cindy, the woman he planned to kill, before he did.

Maya tried to move quicker, forcing herself to ignore the squeaking and rustling of the plastic underfoot. She told herself that if she was right about the killer suffering hearing loss, it didn't matter so much anyway, but even so, she couldn't force herself to simply run through there. She was alone for this, and she only had one chance. She had to be careful.

Maya checked the rooms one by one, opening up the plastic in front of them and sweeping them with her gun in a two-handed grip. She couldn't run the risk that the killer had already dragged his victim into one of those rooms and was strangling her even as Maya walked past.

Yet there was nothing. The rooms seemed empty. The whole *place* seemed empty.

Had Maya made a mistake in moving so cautiously? The moment she'd seen this place, the moment she'd even heard of it, it had seemed obvious that this would be the ambush site, yet what if it wasn't? What if the killer was actually planning to strike closer to Cindy's vehicle, maybe even kill her and shove her in the trunk so that he could drive her to whatever display site he'd picked out?

Had Maya wasted time that she should have been using to race towards the parking lot? That thought terrified her, even as she tried to tell herself that it was a much worse place for a murder. Yes, a parking lot could be quiet if everyone else had left, but she guessed it would also be monitored by cameras, and there was no way of knowing if some other member of staff would be coming down to collect their vehicle.

No, it had to be here. It was the only place that made sense. Maya forced herself to keep looking, to keep checking this space, even though every passing second made her more and more certain that she'd made the wrong choice and should have kept moving. If she got someone killed because she'd made the wrong decision…

Maya heard it then: the muffled sound of someone trying to cry out, the rustling of plastic sheeting and the scrape of wood.

She ran towards the sound, tearing plastic sheets out of the way so that she could cut through the building in the most direct route. Maya wasn't bothered about staying covert now so much as about simply getting there in time.

She got tangled up in one of the sheets for the moment, and it was like being grabbed from every side at once. Every second it took for Maya to disentangle herself was like a wound, because she knew that in those seconds, a woman was getting attacked.

Finally, she broke free and ran forward again. She found herself in a medical bay, where a large, muscled man had what looked like a rubber coated instrument cable pulled tight around the neck of a woman in a nurse's uniform.

The woman was slightly built and short, looking utterly panicked as she scrabbled at the makeshift garotte. Her feet kicked out at anything they could find, as if getting enough purchase would somehow take away the pressure on her neck.

The man had some kind of headphones on his head, but nevertheless, he seemed to hear Maya coming, because he turned towards her as she entered, holding the young woman he was attacking between the two of them like a shield.

"Stay back," the man snarled. He had a heavy featured face and lank dark hair. He was wearing dark jeans and a cheap gray sweatshirt. To Maya, he looked caught between anger and fear. "Don't think I won't kill her."

Maya kept her gun trained on him. She didn't have a clean shot, though. Although the killer was larger than his intended victim, he didn't stand still, but instead used the cable around her throat to yank her around in front of him.

"What's your name?" Maya asked.

"What?" Maya saw him reach up and adjust something on his headphones.

"What's your *name*?" Maya repeated.

"You don't need to know my name, Agent Gray."

Was it supposed to impress Maya that he knew who she was? She'd already worked out that he was listening in on her.

"You might as well tell me. You aren't getting out of here," Maya said.

The killer looked a little angry at that, but then shrugged. "I am, and I'm taking Cindy here with me."

"I can't let you do that," Maya said, keeping her gun levelled.

He let out a short laugh then. "You think you can stop me? What are you going to do? Shoot through her? You want that, Cindy?"

Maya saw him slacken off the pressure on the ligature enough that the nurse could take a breath.

"Why are you doing this, Wendel?" she gasped out. "I didn't do anything to you."

The big man jerked savagely on the cable then, making his captive gasp.

"Didn't *do* anything? You humiliated me. You lied to me. You told me again and again that *this* didn't have to ruin my life." He gestured to the headphones. "That all my fears about no woman wanting me were unfounded, because this didn't matter. Then you turned me down. You showed me what a lie it all was."

158

"You're planning to kill someone just because she rejected you, Wendel?" Maya asked, being sure to use his name, just to make it clear that she'd heard it. "You think that's enough of a reason?"

"It's enough for me," Wendel snapped back. "Why shouldn't I?"

"What about your reasons for killing the other women?" Maya asked. "Jenette Hiatt?"

"I tried out for an internship at the radio. She made every day hell for me. It was as though the only way she could be happy was by making other people feel like nothing."

That tallied with what Maya had seen of her.

"And Cynthia Yoo?"

"I begged her to make an exception for me," Wendel said. "I told her how much I needed her implants. That I couldn't go on with just *these*." He gestured to the headphones. "They amplify sound, sure, but all the sound. Do you know what it's like trying to pick out a conversation in a crowded room, or when there's a car backfiring nearby, and I'm not quick enough to turn the volume down?"

"The procedure wouldn't have worked on you, Wendel," Cindy said, and gasped again as Wendel wrenched on the ligature.

"It would have worked. It *had* to work. It was just all of you, laughing at me. Well, you won't be laughing soon."

He started to walk backwards, towards an opening in one of the plastic sheets, dragging the nurse with him.

"I can't let you do that," Maya said. She tried to line up a shot, but it was still impossible to be sure that she wouldn't hit Cindy by mistake.

An awful thought came to her: should she do it anyway? Should she risk it, just to stop the killer before the Moonlight Killer's deadline? To save her sister? As quickly as she thought it, Maya dismissed the idea. She couldn't do something like that, even for Megan, but she couldn't let Wendel get out of her sight, either.

Worse, because he was dragging Cindy now, she was starting to choke again. Maya probably only had a matter of seconds before she fell unconscious, and only a little longer after that before she died. She had to think of something.

An idea came to her, and Maya pointed her weapon at the ceiling.

"What are you-" Wendel began.

Maya fired twice, the sound huge and echoing in the confines of the half-built wing. It even hurt her ears to hear it, but it did far worse with

Wendel. He cried out, putting his hands up to his ears as he let go of the ligature.

Maya ran at him, grabbing for his headphones first and wrenching them from his head. The big man was still groaning in agony at the pain of the amplified gunshot, but he lashed out blindly, the blow catching Maya on the shoulder and sending her reeling back. Her gun went spinning from her hand, off among the plastic sheeting. She tossed Wendel's headphones to one side, but that just gave him time in which to run staggering off into the depths of the plastic sheeting.

Maya wanted to give chase, but she had to pause, kneeling by Cindy, pulling the ligature from around her throat. She heard the nurse take a huge, shuddering breath, her eyes wide.

"Are you all right?" Maya asked her. She couldn't just abandon the nurse, couldn't risk letting her die if Wendel had left her needing medical attention.

Cindy nodded, just barely, and that was enough to send Maya off into the plastic, hunting for Wendel again. He would be trying to get away now, trying to make his way to an exit, so Maya had to hurry. She pushed through the plastic sheeting, trying to catch up.

Maya saw the shadow of something coming towards her and ducked just in time. The shovel Wendel was now holding passed over Maya's head by a matter of inches. Wendel barreled into her, almost knocking Maya down, but Maya managed to spin clear just in time. She slammed into a wooden post, bounced off, and then ducked again as Wendel swung at her once more.

She managed to kick him in the knee, and he grunted, jabbing at her with the shovel, forcing her to keep her distance. He swung at her once more, then plunged back into the sheeting.

Maya went after him, moving at a tangent into the spaces between the plastic sheeting. Maya looked around, hunting for him once more, her heart beating quickly. She should have realized that for a man like Wendel, the only response to a woman trying to stand up to him was to attempt to kill her. Besides, it was the only way for him to get what he wanted. If he could kill Maya first, then he could go back at his leisure to finish Cindy.

Maya knew in that instant which way he would be going. She started to circle around, making her way back towards the spot where she'd left Cindy. If she was too slow now, he might decide that he didn't need to copy the Moonlight Killer's MO precisely for this murder, just finish Cindy with the shovel that he held.

Maya hurried back and saw Wendel there in the treatment space where he'd been attacking Cindy, but there was no sign of the nurse. She'd obviously realized the danger and managed to move off, trying to hide.

Wendel started to move through the disused ward, obviously looking for her, and Maya followed.

She padded along quickly now, making sure that she stayed behind Wendel where he couldn't see her. Since there was no sign that he'd recovered his headphones, she guessed that he couldn't hear her. She hoped so, at least.

Maya moved forward, closing the gap. She could see Wendel ahead, just the other side of another piece of plastic sheeting.

Maya tore it aside and grabbed him, pulling him back while kicking hard at the back of his knee. He went down, and Maya fell with him. He tried to swing the shovel at her, but being this close and with Maya still behind him, there was no leverage. He dropped it instead, and started to buck and thrash, trying to dislodge Maya's grip.

She clung tighter instead, wrapping her arms and legs around him so that she clung to him on the ground like a backpack. Wendel was so strong though that he actually started to get to his feet. He made it halfway, and then flung himself back, straight at one of the wooden posts.

His weight slammed into Maya, and she tasted blood as her head slammed back into the wood. She didn't let go, though. Doing that would just leave her slumped on the ground with Wendel able to turn and attack her. Instead, she clung on for dear life, even as Wendel slammed her against the post a second time.

This time, though, Maya saw an opportunity. Wendel's chin jerked back as he tried to slam her harder, and that gave Maya all the space she needed to get her forearm under his throat. She grabbed the bicep of her other arm, thrust the back of her rear hand behind his head, and squeezed the choke for all she was worth.

This time, Wendel threw himself at the ground, and again, the impact was terrific. It was like being strapped to a boulder as it slammed into the side of a mountain, but Maya didn't relax her grip, even as pain flared through her. She clung on, dragging her elbow back, expanding her chest into the choke to force it deeper.

161

Slowly, she felt Wendel's struggles start to weaken. He fought, hands scrabbling up for her eyes now, but Maya ducked her head and closed her eyes tight. She kept squeezing. All there was in the world was the choke.

She felt the moment when Wendel went limp. Maya had to force herself to let go in that moment, had to tell herself that it was ok. She rolled Wendel off her, struggling out from underneath him and groaning as the pain of being slammed against so many hard surfaces hit home.

She cuffed him, and then fell back.

Maya lay there for a moment or two, feeling satisfaction start to flood through her. She'd done it.

Then the fear hit her. What time was it?

She searched her pockets for her phone, but it must have fallen out somewhere in the struggle. Maya scanned the floor for it, and for a moment, she couldn't spot it. Then her eyes fell on it, and she dove for it, snatching it up. Only a few minutes before midnight.

She opened up the phone. The screen was cracked, and Maya found herself praying that it was working. She called Harris. His voicemail caught the call, but that didn't matter. It wasn't him she was speaking to right now.

"Harris, I've done it. I've caught the guy who killed Jenette Hiatt. His name is Wendel, and I've caught him, you bastard. I know you're listening. I've *caught* him. You murdered one of your bunnies for *nothing.*"

162

CHAPTER THIRTY ONE

Maya was still lying there when the police burst in. Sheriff O'Neil and two of his deputies came running in with their guns drawn. The sheriff looked quite shocked to see Maya and Wendel both there like that.

Maya groaned and forced herself to sit up. Everything about her hurt. "Sheriff O'Neil, *this* is the man who killed Jenette Hiatt and Cynthia Yoo. Given another couple of minutes, he would have killed a nurse here, too."

"We found Cindy on the way in," Sheriff O'Neil said. "She's fine, we're getting her some medical attention."

That was a relief. Maya had done what she could to make sure that the nurse was safe, but she'd still gone after the killer without taking Cindy to safety.

"You look like you could use a little medical attention yourself," Sheriff O'Neil said.

Maya's ribs ached. So did her back and her head. On the other hand, Wendel was coming around.

It occurred to her then that there was a potential problem. They would get him for attempting to murder Cindy. Maybe there would even be enough evidence to prove his connection to Jenette and Cynthia once they delved into his life properly, but there were no guarantees. Maya had gotten a confession, but only she and Cindy had heard it, and with the stress of everything that had happened, it was possible that Cindy might not remember it all.

"It can wait." She moved to the would-be killer. Maya found his headphones and set them back on his head. She saw his face redden with anger as he struggled against the cuffs that held him. He made it all the way up to his knees before Sheriff O'Neil's deputies grabbed his shoulders, holding him in place.

"You bitch! I'll kill you!"

"Like you were going to kill Cindy?" Maya said, deliberately picking a slightly taunting tone. Maybe this wouldn't have worked with someone else, but Maya had a pretty good idea by now about the kind of man that Wendel was. The kind who got so angry over a rejected date that he tried to kill someone wouldn't be able to hold back his anger now, surely?

Maya waited for the outburst, but it seemed in one sense that she'd misjudged him. Rather than reacting angrily, he seemed to fold in on himself. Maya actually saw tears streaking down his cheeks as the full enormity of all of this hit him.

"Yes, I was going to kill her," he said. "You don't know what it's like, being rejected like that, being made to feel like you're some kind of... of *freak*. Jenette was bad enough with all her taunting, her endless bullying. She deserved it."

"Which is why you killed her too," Maya said. She wanted this clear. She wanted it in the open, where there could be no doubt about it.

"Yes, I killed her, too."

"And Dr. Yoo?"

"And Cynthia. She wouldn't help me. I begged her to help me, and she just refused, like it was nothing. Like it wasn't her *fault*."

Maya could almost feel sympathy for him there, on his knees, crying as he confessed, except for what he was confessing to. Even now, he seemed to be trying to make out that this was the fault of his victims, that he hadn't had any choice about it.

"Her fault, Wendel? You're the one who decided to kill a medical pioneer, because she couldn't, *couldn't* help you. You decided to kill a bully, when anyone else would just have gotten her fired. You decided that the best reaction to being rejected was to try to murder the woman in question."

"It wasn't like that," Wendel insisted.

"It was exactly like that," Maya snapped back. She saved her sympathy for his victims. "What's your last name, Wendel? I never found out while you were trying to kill me."

"Andover," he grunted. Maya didn't care about his resentment right then, only that she'd caught him.

"Wendel Andover, you're under arrest for the murders of Jenette Hiatt and Cynthia Yoo, along with the attempted murder tonight."

Maya signaled to the deputies, and they moved to take him away. Sheriff O'Neil looked pleased and held out his hand for her to shake.

"I'm impressed, Agent Gray," he said. "We'll take him in, and make sure he gets everything he deserves."

"And Benny Gibb?" Maya asked. The thought of the PI just walking free didn't sit well with her.

"We'll be charging him with offenses relating to his stalking," Sheriff O'Neil said. "*Now* will you go and get some medical attention?"

Maya nodded, although she had no plans to stay there long. She didn't even plan to stay at her hotel tonight. She wanted to get back to D.C. She wanted to be home, in the knowledge that her boss wasn't going to kick her out of her job.

More than all of that, though, she wanted to wait there for the postcard that she knew was coming. She wanted the release of the woman whose safety she'd earned.

*

From his spot in a small stand of trees, Frank watched the progress of the cop car that was due to transfer Wendel Andover to jail with a mixture of determination and anger. This man had dared to copy him? To try to pin his own petty, *stupid* crimes on him?

Frank had considered a number of ways to do this. He'd rejected trying to strike in the prison itself this time, because security was tighter there than last time. Yes, he could probably have done it, could probably have found someone willing to shank Andover while he was inside for the right bribe, but that seemed too impersonal. He found himself wanting to do this one himself.

He'd also rejecting attacking the car Andover was travelling in. He could have done that, could have taken the whole thing out with an IED if he wanted, or found a way to stop the car and then attacked it with a full arsenal of weaponry. He could have hired a gang to do it for him or sat there with a sniper rifle and picked Wendel Andover off from close to a thousand yards. It had been a while.

Yet Frank didn't want to do any of those things. For a start, they were messy. It wasn't that he cared whether the police lived or died, but he didn't want the additional trouble that would come from it. He didn't want to risk the disruption that might come to his game if dear Maya or her bosses decided that more police deaths made it untenable to keep working with him.

So he'd found a better way.

165

Carefully, Frank drove out of the stand of trees in the car he'd stolen for exactly this purpose. He affixed lights to the roof and sounded his siren, pulling up alongside the police vehicle.

Frank waved them down, flashing a badge from a distance. It was enough, at least, to get them to pull over. Frank pulled over a little past them, then got out, as non-threatening as he could manage to look.

He'd chosen his disguise carefully for this, working with prosthetics and makeup to add years, changing the shape of his face. He wore tinted glasses too. He didn't want to give facial recognition software *anything* to work with.

He'd chosen the uniform carefully, too. People looked at uniforms when they should have been looking at faces. This one was US Marshal Services, and the badge was even real, supplied by a young thief who'd received a postcard at just the right moment.

He approached the cop car carefully, making sure that he showed no threat. One of the officers, a deputy in his forties with a beer gut, got out to greet him.

"Everything ok?" he asked.

"Not even close," Frank said. He changed his voice, of course, adopting a Texan accent. It was always better to be from somewhere else. "The US Marshal Service has received information that this prisoner is in danger, that the Moonlight Killer plans to target him inside the local jail."

"Inside a jail?" the deputy said. "That doesn't seem likely."

"He managed it just a few days ago," Frank said. "Killed a serial killer by the name of Matheson right in his cell. Our theory is that these individuals have some kind of information on him. That's why I've been given orders to take him into marshal custody until his trial."

The deputy looked incredulous at that. "You want to take *our* prisoner?"

"A prisoner arrested by a federal agent," Frank said. "Besides, I have the orders right here."

He passed the cop paperwork that he'd forged quite carefully, giving him all the time in the world to read through them.

"What's the hold up?" the other cop asked. He was a younger deputy, probably barely old enough to join the force, skinny and obviously raw.

"Maybe you can come talk some sense into your partner," Frank suggested. "I have orders for a prisoner transfer right here, but he's taking his sweet time about it."

That was enough to get the other cop out of the car, coming to take a look. Frank let him get close.

"If it's an order, do we have to hand him over?" the younger cop asked.

"I don't know about this," the older one said. "It isn't the way these things are meant to happen."

"It's not a normal situation," Frank said. He gestured to the car. "But I understand. Why don't you go call it in? You'll see."

The older cop nodded and turned back towards the car. That was when Frank hit him with an elbow to the base of the skull, hard enough to send him slumping into unconsciousness. The key when fighting two people was surprise, and to turn it into a fight against one person as quickly as possible. It would have been far more certain if Frank could just kill them both, but for now, it seemed that his sudden strike was enough. The older cop fell, and Frank was already closing the distance on his partner.

The younger cop was too slow to react, caught off guard by the sudden shift into violence. Frank found that people often were. It meant that Frank could get the grip he wanted almost immediately. The cop tried to rip clear, but Frank pulled him in, landing a couple of knees to the body that drove the air out of the young man, doubling him over. That let Frank finish with another vicious elbow to the skull. The younger cop went down just as quickly as his older colleague.

Honestly, it was too easy. People never ceased to disappoint him with how poorly they did. Except for Maya. So far, she was living up to his expectations surprisingly well. It was almost... gratifying.

Frank cuffed the two deputies and picked up the forged order. Best not to leave anything behind that might actually have forensic traces. Taking the cops' keys, he opened up the back of the car, pulling Wendel Andover out of there.

"What is this?" Wendel said. "Some kind of breakout?"

"No, Wendel," Frank said, and now the cops were out of the picture, he reverted to the coldness of his normal voice. "This is not a breakout."

Maybe it was the look in his eyes, but Frank could see the fear starting to spread over Wendel's face like a stain.

167

"W-what is this? What are you doing?"

"What did *you* do?" Frank countered. "You thought that you could have people blame *me* for your handiwork? You thought that if you just killed women on the night of the full moon, that was *enough*? As if you understand the meaning? As if you *get* why it has to happen?"

Frank saw the fear turn to terror, and Wendel tried to run, even cuffed as he was. Frank tripped him easily. As Wendel tried to scramble back to his feet, Frank knelt on his back, holding him there.

He took out the strangling rope and wrapped it around Wendel's throat.

"Please," Wendel begged. "I'll give you anything you want."

"But the only thing I want is you dead," Frank replied.

He pulled the rope taut.

"Did you enjoy it, this moment?" Frank asked him. "Did the purity of it touch you the way it should? Or was it just something you got out of the way to make sure that someone was dead? It was, wasn't it? You didn't see the truth of it at all."

This was a better moment than when he'd done this to Carmel. This was something planned. Something he'd anticipated since the start of all this. It meant that he could savor the thrashing, the slow settling into unconsciousness. He could savor every moment of this imposter's death, every twitch, every gasp in a way that no one else truly could.

Although he'd heard that Maya had strangled this one too. Maybe they were more alike than she wanted to think. Maybe she would truly appreciate this moment.

Maybe one day, he would show her firsthand.

CHAPTER THIRTY TWO

Maya went into work still feeling worried about what her reception would be, yet the moment she saw Harris's face, she knew everything was going to be ok. Her boss didn't look angry anymore. Instead, he had the familiar congratulatory look that Maya had seen plenty of times before when she'd finished cases.

"Well done, Gray," he said, patting her on the back. It was a big change from the way he'd been just a day ago. "I got your message. I assume it was the Moonlight Killer you were insulting, and not me?"

Maya suspected that it had been a little of both, there at the end, but this didn't seem like a good moment to say it.

"I assumed that he would be listening in, sir," she said. "I think we *all* have to assume that he's listening."

Her boss's expression lost some of its good humor then. "We're going to catch that bastard, whatever it takes."

Maya understood the determination, but she was worried that in Harris's case, it might be starting to tip over into obsession.

"Does it at least mean that I can stay on this?" Maya said.

Harris paused, appearing to consider it. "I still don't like that we're in the hands of a man who has killed one of his captives for no reason, but for now, I don't see any better options. You're still working the case. I sorted things out with the Pollock prison incident. Just don't go too far, Gray. There are still rules."

"I know that, sir," Maya said. Unfortunately, right now, the rules that mattered most were the ones being set by the Moonlight Killer. "I'll be more careful. For now, though, there's something I need to do."

She walked off and made a call. Maya was almost surprised, after everything that she'd done, when Marco picked up.

"Hey Maya, what do you need from me?" There was still a wary note in his voice. After the way their last conversation had gone, Maya didn't blame him.

"I don't need anything," Maya said. "I'm just calling to say that I'm sorry. I'm not interrupting anything, am I?"

"I cleared up the murders yesterday," Marco said. "But obviously, things don't stop in the big city."

"*Big* city?" Maya said. "Cleveland?"

Marco laughed along with her.

"I really am sorry though," Maya said. "I got so wrapped up in everything that I couldn't see past it. I couldn't even enjoy one evening out with you without it turning into a work thing."

"That's my fault too," Marco said. "Maybe it just wasn't the right time."

"It's not your fault," Maya insisted. "Look... maybe we could try it again sometime? If you haven't been too turned off by the obsessive agent routine?"

"It would take more than that," Marco assured her. "And it would be good to try again. But maybe no work this time?"

It was Maya's turn to laugh. "I'll do my best. So I'll see you soon."

"Very soon, I hope," Marco said.

They hung up, leaving Maya feeling a lot better about the way things stood between them. There was no denying that she'd treated Marco poorly, that she'd used him as little more than a resource, when he'd been thinking of her in very different terms. Maya resolved to do better next time around.

She was still thinking about Marco when Reyes ran up.

"Gray, get over here. A postcard has come."

Maya ran over to her desk, where a small crowd of agents had gathered. A postcard sat on it, presumably delivered through the FBI's internal mail. Harris was standing over it, but at least the agents around her desk moved aside to let Maya through. Maya took the postcard by its corners, seeing a picture of a happy bunny playing outside a large red barn. She flipped it over and started to read aloud, so the others could hear.

"'Dearest Maya, congratulations on finding Jenette Hiatt's killer. You were very resourceful. Accordingly, a bunny will be released at the coordinates at the top of the postcard. Bring your fellow agents if you wish. I shall not be there.

I also wish you to know that the bunny who died did so thanks to her own foolishness, not due to anything you and yours did. She tried to spring her hutch, and it was necessary to make an example to the others.

Oh, and when you find out what I did to Wendel, don't be *too* disappointed. I was very gentle with the police, just for you.'"

A slew of emotions rushed through Maya, unanswered questions coming to her far too quickly to process all at once. What did he mean that Carmel had tried to spring her hutch? She'd attempted to escape? Maya found herself hoping in that moment that Megan wouldn't try to do anything brave. She couldn't stand the thought of her sister ending up like that.

Then there was the other question.

"What happened to Wendel Andover?" Maya asked Harris.

"We're calling Albany now," he said. Even as he did it, an agent came up to him and whispered to him. Maya saw the shift in his expression, the cold fury replacing his uncertainty. "That *bastard*. He, or someone he employed, has just attacked the police car transporting Wendel Andover to jail. They knocked out two police officers, and then strangled Andover."

The same way that he'd had the killer in her last case murdered. Was he planning on killing *all* the people Maya found?

"We should check on the kid who killed Anne Postmartin," Maya said. "It's possible that this guy might target him too."

"I'll have someone check," Harris said. He was staring at the postcard. "No riddles this time. No games."

"Maybe he's trying to make up for killing Carmel," Maya suggested.

"He's trying to make it up to *you*," Harris said. "He's getting obsessed with you. That's dangerous, Gray."

Maya knew exactly how dangerous, because she was the only one there even now who knew who they were dealing with.

"I just have to hope that it will prove more dangerous for him," Maya said. "For now, though, we need to find the woman he's let go."

*

They sped out to the location in a convoy that included Maya, Harris, a tactical team and an ambulance, all speeding through the countryside fast enough that Maya had to cling to her seat. It made sense to move this fast, though, when the Moonlight Killer's last two captives had been in rough shape by the time that they'd found them.

They got closer to the coordinates, not far outside D.C., obviously another show of contrition by the Moonlight Killer in picking such a convenient location. Maya didn't believe that contrition for a moment. It was just another way to try to manipulate her.

Even so, as soon as she saw the abandoned barn, she knew it was the right place. It was large, and red, even if it was a long way from being in pristine condition. It looked as though a stiff breeze might have blown it down, with holes in the side and a roof that was only part there. It clearly hadn't been used in a long time.

They rushed to the barn, parking up in front of it, not even trying to be stealthy. Speed counted for more here. They piled out of their vehicles, with Maya hurrying to keep up with Harris. The deputy director was striding through it all, calling out orders.

"You three, secure the perimeter. The rest of you, sweep the barn. Paramedics stand by."

The tactical team swept forward into the barn. Maya didn't wait for an invitation, but instead followed them, gun held ready in case this all turned out to be another of the Moonlight Killer's ambushes.

The barn was mostly empty, with even the most rusted machinery cleared out long ago. There, tied to a post at its center, sat a young woman in a gray jumpsuit. She was slightly built and blonde haired, obviously dehydrated and terrified looking.

Maya made to move forward, but a member of the tactical team held an arm up.

"We need to check for traps first."

Waiting while they started to do that was an agony, creeping forward, step by step, towards the young woman there. She obviously looked frightened by the whole thing, and Maya realized that the best thing she could do in that situation was reassure her.

"We're here to save you," she said. "We'll get you out of here as soon as we know it's safe. What's your name?"

"Katya," the young woman said. "My name is Katya."

"Katya, I'm Agent Gray. You can call me Maya."

"Maya?" Katya said. "Megan's sister?"

That was enough to make Maya rush forward, in spite of the potential for traps.

"You know my sister?" Maya said, as she cut Katya loose. Paramedics were already rushing in, bringing a stretcher with them.

172

"We'll need to get her back to the ambulance and give her fluids," one of them said.

Harris was there then. He obviously had as many questions as Maya did. The difference was that the paramedics couldn't gainsay him.

"Did you see anything?" he asked. "Do you remember *anything* about where you were?"

"I...," Katya nodded slightly. "I've always been good at knowing where I am. I think I know which direction he took me to get here. I *kind of* know how far."

Maya saw the hope on Harris's face then, mixed in with the determination to know more. "And we have some forensic results that may prove helpful. Taken together, we might actually have a chance to *find* this guy."

Maya felt a surge of hope at that, but there was worry mixed in with it. Was Harris really going to mount another raid? Walk into what might prove to be another trap?

"Later," the paramedic said. "You can talk to her later. For now, we should get her checked out."

Maya saw Harris relent, and the paramedics started to move Katya onto a stretcher. To her surprise, the young woman reached out to catch hold of Maya's arm, pulling her closer. Close enough to whisper.

"I have a message... from your sister."

NOW AVAILABLE!

GIRL FOUR: LURED
(A Maya Gray FBI Suspense Thriller —Book 4)

12 cold cases. 12 kidnapped women. One diabolical serial killer. In this riveting suspense thriller, a brilliant FBI agent faces a deadly challenge: decipher the mystery before each one is murdered.

In the Maya Gray series (which begins with Book #1—GIRL ONE: MURDER) FBI Special Agent Maya Gray, 39, has seen it all. She's one of BAU's rising stars and the go-to agent for hard-to-crack serial cases. When she receives a handwritten postcard promising to release 12 kidnapped women if she will solve 12 cold cases, she assumes it's a hoax.

Until the note mentions that, among the captives, is her missing sister.

Maya, shaken, is forced to take it seriously. The cases she's up against are some of the most difficult the FBI has ever seen. But the terms of his game are simple: if Maya solves a case, he will release one of the girls.

And if she fails, he will end a life.

In GIRL FOUR: LURED, bodies are found with a lone jigsaw puzzle piece left atop them, the victims of a serial killer.

What could the meaning be? What puzzle is he trying to complete?

But time is running out, and Maya's sister is in danger. Can she put the pieces together in time to save the next victim?

A complex psychological crime thriller full of twists and turns and packed with heart-pounding suspense, the MAYA GRAY mystery series will make you fall in love with a brilliant new female protagonist and keep you turning pages late into the night. It is a perfect addition for fans of Robert Dugoni, Rachel Caine, Melinda Leigh or Mary Burton.

Books #5 and #6—GIRL FIVE: BOUND and GIRL SIX: FORSAKEN—are also available.

Molly Black

Debut author Molly Black is author of the MAYA GRAY FBI suspense thriller series, comprising six books (and counting); and the RYLIE WOLF FBI suspense thriller series, comprising three books (and counting).

An avid reader and lifelong fan of the mystery and thriller genres, Molly loves to hear from you, so please feel free to visit www.mollyblackauthor.com to learn more and stay in touch.

BOOKS BY MOLLY BLACK

MAYA GRAY MYSTERY SERIES
GIRL ONE: MURDER (Book #1)
GIRL TWO: TAKEN (Book #2)
GIRL THREE: TRAPPED (Book #3)
GIRL FOUR: LURED (Book #4)
GIRL FIVE: BOUND (Book #5)
GIRL SIX: FORSAKEN (Book #6)

RYLIE WOLF FBI SUSPENSE THRILLER
FOUND YOU (Book #1)
CAUGHT YOU (Book #2)
SEE YOU (Book #3)

Made in United States
Troutdale, OR
04/20/2024

19313741R00116